KU-530-712

'When does Lucy have to leave.'

'Today. Now. As soon as I can arrange it.' And that was when Kate realised the implications. By ambulance. The usual driver, Charlie, had retired and just left on his lifetime trip. There was no one else with any training to come with her, and she really needed some back-up for this trip… There was no one with any medical knowledge—except the man from her past who'd flown in this morning to see her.

Rory was the last person she wanted to spend twenty-four hours locked in an ambulance truck with.

She turned away and looked into the room where Lucy lay. Maybe it wouldn't be too bad. Maybe what she'd felt for him when she'd been sweet sixteen and besotted enough to practically force him to make love to her would be different.

Of course it would. He was ten years older now. That made him twenty-eight, and with his job the life experiences would age anyone, so he'd probably have changed, put on city weight, look a lot older. She'd be fine.

But when the driver's door opened and Rory climbed in behind the wheel—all six feet four of him—Kate had to shake her head at her preposterous predictions. There was no doubt the guy was a serious hunk, with a wicked twinkle a long way from surly.

She couldn't help the flare in her stomach, or the illicit pleasure of just looking for a long, slow heartbeat at him.

No wonder she hadn't been able to forget him.

A mother to five sons, **Fiona McArthur** is an Australian midwife who loves to write. Mills & Boon® Medical™ Romance gives Fiona the scope to write about all the wonderful aspects of adventure, romance, medicine and midwifery that she feels so passionate about—as well as an excuse to travel! So, now that the boys are older, her husband Ian and youngest son Rory are off with Fiona to meet new people, see new places, and have wonderful adventures. Fiona's website is at www.fionamcarthur.com

Recent titles by the same author:

PREGNANT MIDWIFE: FATHER NEEDED
  Lyrebird Lake Maternity
THE MIDWIFE'S LITTLE MIRACLE
  Lyrebird Lake Maternity
THE MIDWIFE'S NEW-FOUND FAMILY
  Lyrebird Lake Maternity
THEIR SPECIAL-CARE BABY

MIDWIFE
IN A MILLION

BY
FIONA McARTHUR

All the characters in this book have no existence outside
the imagination of the author, and have no relation
whatsoever to anyone bearing the same name or names.
They are not even distantly inspired by any individual
known or unknown to the author, and all the incidents
are pure invention.

All Rights Reserved including the right of reproduction
in whole or in part in any form. This edition is published
by arrangement with Harlequin Enterprises II BV/S.à.r.l.
The text of this publication or any part thereof may
not be reproduced or transmitted in any form or by
any means, electronic or mechanical, including
photocopying, recording, storage in an information
retrieval system, or otherwise, without the written
permission of the publisher.

® and TM are trademarks owned and used by the
trademark owner and/or its licensee. Trademarks marked
with ® are registered with the United Kingdom Patent
Office and/or the Office for Harmonisation in the
Internal Market and in other countries.

First published in Great Britain 2009
Large Print edition 2010
Harlequin Mills & Boon Limited,
Eton House, 18-24 Paradise Road,
Richmond, Surrey TW9 1SR

© Fiona McArthur 2009

ISBN: 978 0 263 21106 1

Harlequin Mills & Boon policy is to use papers that are
natural, renewable and recyclable products and made
from wood grown in sustainable forests. The logging and
manufacturing process conform to the legal environmental
regulations of the country of origin.

Printed and bound in Great Britain
by CPI Antony Rowe, Chippenham, Wiltshire

MIDWIFE
IN A MILLION

20037276

MORAY COUNCIL
LIBRARIES &
INFORMATION SERVICES

Dedicated to my husband, Ian,
my caring and compassionate paramedic,
and my own true hero.

CHAPTER ONE

RORY MCIVER stepped thankfully from the RFDS aircraft he'd hitched a ride with. It hadn't been one of the smoothest flights he'd ever been on. Maybe he should have driven from Perth but it had been such a hectic couple of weeks that the idea of driving three thousand kilometres on a whim didn't do it for him.

He bent to scoop a little of the red earth he'd watched pass below his window for hours, let it run through his fingers, then allowed the wind to blow the soil from his palm. He looked around. He never thought he'd return.

Even early in the morning on the airstrip the

hot wind wrapped around him like an electric blanket on high, that all enveloping heat that only Western Australia's Kimberley could offer, a heat he hadn't felt for ten years and savoured now.

He touched his shirt pocket and gripped the bulkiness of his wallet in that habit he'd acquired since she'd sent the damn letter all that time ago. Enough!

As the plane bumped away on the dirt strip a cattle dog barked and the dog's lanky owner tipped his finger under his hat in greeting. 'G'day, Rory. Long time, no see.'

Here was a person who hadn't changed. 'Smiley.' Rory nodded to the cowboy leaning against the battered truck. 'Good of you to meet me.' They shook hands and Rory threw his swag in the back where a cloud of red soil smothered it as it landed. He smiled wryly and opened the passenger door against the wind.

When the spinning top of a whirly wind tried to climb in with him he wondered about the implications of the strong breeze.

Smiley pushed himself off the truck and slid behind the wheel to start the engine. 'I wondered how long it would take you after Kate turned up,' Smiley drawled in that remembered way and drew a smile from Rory until the words sank in.

Rory grimaced. Well, apparently not long. 'I read in the newspaper that her father's sick. So she's been gone a long time, too?'

'Hmm. Left the same year as you. Went to school in Perth.' Smiley grunted and let off the handbrake. 'She's back to spend time with him but flies down to the station township a few days a week to relieve Sophie.'

Smiley glanced at a small four-wheel drive vehicle under a lean-to in the corner of the paddock and Rory gathered it was Kate's. 'She works at the clinic, and delivers the babies that drop in from the camps, as well as emergencies.' Smiley shook his head. 'I hear the old man isn't happy she's working here at all.'

Seems Lyle Onslow hadn't changed then. Malignant old sod.

'Her father was never happy.'

'He's dying.' Smiley turned to look at him and they both thought about that. Lyle was a hard man, and not always fair, but no doubt Saint Peter would sort that one out shortly.

Smiley shrugged the old man's problems away and slipped another matchstick into his mouth to chew. His lips barely moved but the matchstick danced at the edge of his lips in a skill passed down from Smiley's father. It brought back the good memories for Rory and there'd been many of those.

'So you told her you're coming?' Smiley said around the match.

No, Rory thought. He closed his eyes and the sleepless night he'd spent trying to work out how to do that hung heavily behind his lids. 'Try and keep a damper on that news, mate, until I get a chance.'

Smiley snorted, the closest he came to a laugh. 'Keep a damper on it? Here?' Smiley took the matchstick out and pointed it at Rory. 'The airwaves've been hummin' since your plane left Perth.'

Rory supposed he'd known that—just blocked it out—and he'd have to deal with the fact that he'd broken his promise when he saw her.

When he saw her. He didn't know how he felt about seeing the woman who'd dumped him after promising to wait. Had never answered his letters. Had apparently been the cause of heartbreak and suffering for his parents, who had shown her nothing but kindness when her mother died.

He needed more time, or would there never

be enough time between them? Now he'd almost achieved his life's goal he'd finally realised he couldn't move on until he'd settled the past.

'How's Sophie?'

Smiley's sister was the antithesis of her brother. Bubbly and extrovert, she bossed Smiley mercilessly and her dour brother just shrugged. There'd been a time the four of them had done everything together out on the sprawling million acres of Jabiru Station—another thing Kate's father hadn't liked, his daughter knocking about with the hired help.

'Nagging as usual,' Smiley said but there was pride in his voice and he elaborated, unusual for him, as if he sensed Rory's need for a change of subject. 'Now she's working at the clinic with…' He shot him a quick glance.

…with Kate, Rory completed in his mind.

'Anyway, having help means Sophie gets some time off for a change,' Smiley went on.

'So she's good. She's getting tips on baby-catching, she calls it, and thinkin' of doing her midwifery.' He looked back at the road. 'When do you go back?'

Kate the teacher for Sophie? Of course she'd changed. What did he expect? That she'd still think he, Rory, held the answers to the universe?

'I've a week off. I'll stay over at the Hilton until RFDS can pick me up in a couple of days.'

The Hilton was the town's tongue-in-cheek name for the extremely run down boarding house presided over by a tough ex-army nurse, Betty Shultz. Shultzie swore she'd never leave Jabiru Township, then again, Shultzie swore, loudly and often, all the time.

Her Hilton was nothing like the chain of exclusive hotels of the same name; her establishment was bare minimum and held together by pieces of wood nailed over the top of other pieces of wood.

'How was Charlie's retirement party?'

'Good food,' Smiley said. 'Don't suppose you'd want his job?'

After flogging himself to higher and higher levels until last month's appointment? Volunteer ambulance in the bush instead of Deputy Commissioner of the entire state? Actually, it held some attraction. Back on the road instead of budget meetings and troubleshooting.

'No. Afraid not.'

They didn't speak again until they drove past the huge cattle yards on the outskirts and pulled up opposite the rundown hotel in the main street of Jabiru Township, population a hundred and fifty through the week, three hundred— mostly ringers and cowboys—on the weekend. Town, sweet town.

He looked around. A big change from Perth city.

Another whirly wind scooted past Rory as he

lifted his swag out of the back and he glanced at the pale sky for the first streaks of cloud. Not yet.

He thumped the roof and Smiley lifted his hand and drove away. Rory watched the truck until it disappeared in a ball of dust and wondered if he could change his mind and ride it back out to the airstrip.

He'd never run from a challenge before. Funny how attractive that thought was right now, but only for a moment.

Well, he'd arrived. He needed to stop making such a big deal of a visit home. It wasn't as if he had family here any more. He squashed that bitterness away too. The rest—meaning his reaction to Kate—would have to take care of itself.

He looked at the mostly boarded shops in the deserted street. It wasn't like Kate's father's homestead and the home station where he'd grown up, but in the years since he'd been to the commercial part of Jabiru not much had changed.

Except the collateral damage he'd caused to his family by his liaison with Kate.

Kate Onslow was born into the pilot's seat of an aeroplane; luckily, because it made the distance she needed to cover so ridiculously easy.

The two-hour drive between Jabiru Homestead and Jabiru Township was dust all the way and to fly cut the distance down to twenty minutes. Her great-grandfather had settled on the station a hundred years ago and when the township had grown exponentially her grandfather had built a new homestead away from the madding crowds. Though a hundred people didn't seem 'madding' to Kate, she could understand the improvement in position for the family headquarters.

The new Jabiru Homestead, many-gabled, en-circled by verandas and sprawled over an acre, nestled below a range of ochre mountains that bordered the Timor Sea; the peaks gave water and provided glorious waterholes and a lush rainforest pocket, and all only a short distance from the sparseness around the house.

The old homestead at Jabiru Township that she could see in the distance now from the air, held the hospital clinic, the pharmacy, the one-roomed library of donated books and the garage for the town's only four-wheel drive ambulance truck.

As she closed in on her destination Kate saw the Royal Flying Doctor plane take off from the town strip and her heart rate dropped in a swoop as if she'd flown through a sudden wind shift, something her aircraft had been doing all flight, but this internal up-draught made her sick to the stomach.

She'd had three radio calls already to tell her Rory McIver was coming to town to see her.

Last month it had been hard enough to come

back and face her belligerent father and the reality of his illness but that paled in comparison with Rory's unexpected visit.

She'd been able to face the idea of coming home because she'd known her father would never change her mind about anything again. But Rory? Once he'd been the world to her.

She would just have to survive this too. Her independence would help her survive it. The sudden sting of threatening tears she ignored—they never came to anything. She hadn't cried since all that had happened ten years ago and the lies. But the emotional turbulence had started and she hadn't even seen him. She was a big girl now and not some needy teenager with an adolescent crush on the manager's son.

Kate took a deep breath and straightened her shoulders. Too many years she'd spent telling herself she needed to stand on her own, rely on herself, be strong, and that determination would not be undermined by a man who had been out of her life for a long time. What did he want to see her for now, anyway?

Kate stripped Rory's intrusion from her mind and concentrated on her descent because that was her strength. Single-minded concentration on what needed to be done. But, as soon as the plane grounded, as soon as room for distraction arrived, the thoughts returned to stick like the plane's wheels to the ruts on the strip.

She gritted her teeth and secured her aircraft but the worry nagged at her all the way to town in her vehicle. Nagged her through the first half hour at work, right up until sixteen-year-old Lucy Bolton presented with the worst case of indigestion she'd had in her life.

Jabiru Township Clinic serviced the small town set in the baked earth at the edge of the station's southern mountain ranges, a place that hid lush waterholes and settlements, plus far-flung aboriginal communities and out camps for the station. If the situation was dire, the doctor might be able to fly in once a week—unfortunately he'd been in yesterday.

Kate took one look at Lucy and put her to bed in the four bed ward. 'Under those covers, young lady. No arguments. Where's your mother?'

Lucy was a big-boned, hardworking girl whose mother leased one of the four pubs in town from Kate's father. Usually happy-go-lucky and fun, Kate knew Lucy wasn't one to complain. They bred them tough out here—had to—it was a long way to twentieth century medicine.

'Mum's tired.' Lucy sat gingerly on the edge of the bed and kicked off her shoes. 'There was a big outfit in town yesterday and I didn't want to wake her.' Lucy sighed as she rested her head back on the pillow and closed her eyes. 'The queer thing is, Kate,' she whispered, 'I haven't eaten a thing 'cause I feel so rotten, so how can I have indigestion?'

'That's not good.' Kate stared down at the young girl and in a swirl of memories saw herself. 'Poor you.' She stroked her hair. She saw the slight puffiness around the eyes, the tiredness, that protective maternal hand that crept over her stomach. Her voice dropped. 'Any chance you're pregnant, Luce?'

Lucy's eyes flew open and the sudden fear in the young girl's face was enough confirmation. Kate sighed under her breath for the loss of youth coming Lucy's way and a smidgen for the prick of envy. She wished she'd had the sense to ask for help like Lucy had.

Though in Kate's day Mrs Schulz mightn't have been as easy to approach as Kate or Sophie would be, even if Kate had been able to get all the way to the township from the home station.

She stroked Lucy's shoulder. 'Everything will

be fine. I'll just take your blood pressure, poppet. You don't look well to me either.'

By the time Kate had done a full physical assessment the window shutters were banging against the walls outside and the howl of the wind was clearly audible. Kate barely noticed it as her concern grew for the young woman in front of her.

The flying doctor would have to come back and pick her up because there was no way she could manage Lucy here. And there was no way she wanted to because she knew what it could cost.

The pregnancy test proved positive but Kate hadn't needed that; she could clearly hear the heartbeat from Lucy's little passenger inside and she was more worried about the dangerously high levels of protein she found in the specimen of Lucy's urine.

Lucy's uterus could be felt midway between

her belly button and the bottom of her sternum, which meant she'd been hiding her secret for about seven months. Around eight weeks too early to birth, if the baby was growing well. Eight weeks to go!

Kate closed her eyes against the memories that wanted to surface. Right when the trouble had hit her all those years ago. She shook the unwanted thoughts away, not least because she didn't want to jinx Lucy.

Unless Kate was mistaken, Lucy's blood pressure would ensure labour happened soon anyway, and Kate knew how fragile premmie babies were. Not standard procedure around here, three thousand kilometres from Perth.

That was, of course, if Lucy wasn't in labour already and didn't know it. 'You're not having any tummy pains are you, Luce?'

Lucy shook her head carefully. 'Just this headache and rotten indigestion that's killing me.'

It isn't indigestion, Kate thought—it's your body telling you something is very wrong. At least Lucy had listened. Kate poured a small tumbler of antacid, more for comfort, and gave it to her. 'Sip on this, Luce. I need to talk to the doctor on the radio.'

Five minutes later Kate lifted the headphones from her ears and looked at them. No way could they do that. She settled the pads on her ears again and, strangely, the action had calmed her nerves. 'Say again,' she said, but there was little hope it would sound different this time.

'Medication and transfer. If I were you I'd transfer her today. The storm's a big one. The only way to transport is on the ground. If you decide to go you'll have to take her out by road before it rains again and we'll fly her from Derby. Or you could sit on her for another twenty-four hours with those symptoms and pray.'

Kate closed her eyes. 'It's six hundred kilo-metres of corrugations. What if she gets worse on the trip?' Kate had another, more practical thought and her eyes widened. 'What if she goes into labour?'

'You could hope she doesn't deliver.' Mac Dawson had been obstetric registrar when Kate had been a newly graduated midwife at Perth General. Now an obstetrician in Perth, Mac respected her knowledge and she knew he cared about her predicament. But he couldn't do anything about their options. There was nothing else he could suggest. 'You should have stayed with me in Perth.'

Kate rolled her eyes, glad he couldn't see her. He'd asked her out a couple of times and Kate knew he'd have liked to have pursued their re-lationship if she'd been interested. She should have been but wasn't. Mac's pursuit had been a factor in her choice to work at one of the smaller hospitals in the suburbs of Perth after graduation.

Mac went on. 'Her first baby, Kate. It's your call but I'm sure you'd prefer early labour to an eclampsia out there while you wait for the storm to pass. The weather could set in for days and your strip will wash out. It'll get tricky if she's as unstable as you think and the roads are cut.'

Mac was right. She'd just needed to hear it twice. Road it was then. 'Thanks for that, Mac. I'll get back to you when I talk to her parents.'

'Hear from you soon, then. Don't forget to give me a ring when you get in so I can be sure you made it.'

Kate pulled the earphones from her head slowly and walked back to her patient via the drug cupboard. She reached for what she needed, along with the tray of intravenous cannulas, and set it down on the table beside the bed.

Lucy had fallen into an uneasy doze and every

now and then her arm twitched in her sleep. Kate rechecked her blood pressure and the figures made her wince.

'Lucy.' Kate held the girl's wrist as she counted her pulse. Lucy's eyes flickered open. 'I have to put a drip in your arm, poppet, and give you some drugs to bring your blood pressure down. Then I'll ring your mum. The doctor says you have to go to Derby at least. Probably Perth.'

Lucy's eyes opened wide and the apprehension in them made Kate squeeze her hand again. She looked so frightened. Kate had been frightened too.

'It's okay, I'll come with you most of the way but you'll have to stay there until after your baby is born.'

'Mum doesn't know I'm having a baby.' They both looked down at Lucy's difficult to distinguish stomach.

Kate remembered this all too well except she hadn't had a mother. Just a ranting, wild-eyed father who'd bundled her off to strangers before anyone else found out.

'We'll have to tell her, but no one else needs to know just yet. This is serious, Luce. You could get really sick and so could your baby. I'm worried about you so we have no choice.'

Lucy slumped back in the bed and closed her eyes and two big silver tears slid down her cheeks. 'I understand. Will you tell Mum?'

Kate looked down at Lucy's soft round cheeks and her hand lifted and smoothed the limp hair back off her forehead. Poor Lucy. 'If you want me to. Of course I will.'

The next half an hour made Kate wonder how some people could be so lucky. Lucy's mother sagged at the news but straightened with a determined glint in her eye. 'My poor baby. To think she'd been worrying about upsetting me when I'd be more worried about her. Here was me thinking all sorts of terrible things when now I can see why she's been so quiet lately. And you say she's sick?' Mary Bolton stared at Kate hard. 'How sick?'

'It used to be called toxemia of pregnancy. Her blood pressure's high and dangerous, for both her and her baby. I'm worried she could have a fit if it gets too high. They want her flown to Perth.'

Mary stared out of the window and then back at Kate. 'I had that 'clampsia thing. Scared the pants off the old man when he woke up and the bed was shaking, with me staring at him like a stunned rabbit unable to speak.' Mary shrugged. 'Or so he said—that was just before Lucy was born,' Mary said matter-of-factly and Kate's stomach dropped. Maternal history of eclampsia as well? So her mother had progressed to fitting. Kate closed her eyes. More risk for Lucy.

Mary glanced out of the window and frowned. 'But the Flying Doctor won't be able to fly in this weather.'

Kate looked out of the window to see what she already knew. The sky was heavy and purpling now. 'I know. We'll have to take her by road to Derby. Unless the weather clears further west and they can fly in and meet us at one of the stations along the way.'

Mary looked down at her daughter, then at Kate. 'You must be worried, Kate, if you can't wait here a day or two.'

'I am.'

Mary grimaced. 'We're lucky you're here. I'll have to arrange for someone to take over the pub and mind the other kids, then I'll follow. My sister lives in Derby. When does Lucy have to go?'

'Today. Now. As soon as I can arrange it.' And that was when Kate realised the implications. By ambulance. The usual driver, Charlie, had retired and just left on his lifetime dream holiday. There was no one else with any training to come with her, and she really needed some backup for this trip…

Sophie would be needed here and there was no one with any medical knowledge except— the second highest qualified paramedic in the state—she'd heard he'd got the Deputy job. The man from her past who'd flown in this morning to see her.

Rory was the last person she wanted to spend twenty-four hours locked in an ambulance truck with.

She turned away and looked into the room where Lucy lay. Maybe it wouldn't be too bad. Maybe what she'd felt for him when she'd been sweet sixteen and besotted enough to practically force him to make love to her would be different.

Of course it would. He was ten years older

now—that made him twenty-eight. With his job the on-road experiences would age anyone, so he'd probably have changed, put on city weight, look a lot older. She'd be fine.

The call came in just as Rory finished unpacking. Betty knocked like a machine gun on his door and Rory flinched from too many sudden call situations in the city. Maybe he did need this break away from work.

Betty in a battledress shirt and viciously creased trousers was a scary thing as she stood ramrod-straight outside his door, and he wondered if he should salute her.

He opened the door wider, but gingerly, because the handle felt as if it was going to come off in his hand. The place was falling apart.

The fierce expression on Shultzie's face made him wonder if he was going to be put through an emergency fire drill. 'Yes, ma'am?'

'Kate Onslow's on the phone for you. Best take it in the hall quick smart.'

He moved fast enough even for Shultzie to be satisfied.

CHAPTER TWO

RORY parked the ambulance outside the front door of the clinic and climbed the steps to the wooden veranda. His boots clunked across the dusty wood as the wind whipped his shirt against his body.

He could remember riding out to one of the station fences in weather like this to shift cattle with his father, a big man then that no horse could throw, with the gusty wind in their faces and the sky a cauldron above their heads. He could remember them eyeing the forks of lightning on the horizon with respect. And he remembered his father telling him to forget about any future with Kate Onslow. That it wasn't his place. She was out of his league.

His feeling of betrayal that his own father hadn't thought him good enough for Kate either had remained until his dad had been fired not long after Rory had left, after twenty years of hard work, and his dad's motive became clearer.

Lyle Onslow had a lot to answer for. The problem was Rory had always loved Kate. Not just because she'd hero-worshipped him since she'd started at the tiny station school but because he could see the flame inside her that her own father had wanted to stamp out.

He understood the insecurities she'd fought against and how she refused to be cold and callous like Lyle Onslow. She'd been a brave but lonely little girl with a real kindness for those less fortunate that never tipped into pity and her father had hated her for it.

It wasn't healthy or Christian, but Rory hoped

Kate's father suffered a bit before the end. He shoved the bitter thoughts back into the dark place they belonged, along with the guilt that he'd caused his parents' misfortunes.

No wonder he'd never wanted to come back after Kate's letter. Kate, who hadn't needed him for what seemed a lifetime but needed him now.

The lightning flickered and a few drops of rain began to form circular puffs of dust in the road. 'Lovely weather for ducks,' he muttered out loud—his mother's favourite saying and one he hadn't said for years—to shake off the gloomy thoughts that sat like icy water on his soul.

He pushed open the door and walked down the hall to the clinic.

Rory's first sight of Kate winded him as if he'd run into one of those shutters banging in the street on the way.

He'd tried to picture this moment so many times

on the way but she looked so different from what he'd imagined and a whole lot more distant.

She was dressed in fitted tan trousers that hugged her slim hips and thighs above soft-skinned riding boots. The white buttoned shirt just brushed her trim waist and an elusive curve of full breast peeped from the shifting vee of her neckline and then disappeared, a bit like his breath, as she turned to face him. He lifted his gaze.

Thick dark hair still pulled back in a ponytail, no sign yet of grey, but ten years had added a definition to her beauty—womanly beauty—yet the set of her chin was tougher and steadier and she'd probably reach his chin now so she didn't look as fragile as he'd remembered.

Lord, she was beautiful.

He'd have liked to have sat somewhere out of sight and just studied her to see the changes and nuances of this Kate he didn't know. Breathe in the truth that he was here, beside her, and acknowledge she still touched him on a level no other woman had reached. But his training kicked in. There'd be time for that later.

'Rory,' she said but she was talking to the wall behind his head, which was a shame because he ached with real hunger for her to look at him. 'Thank you for offering to help.' She barely paused for breath, as if to eliminate any possibility of other topics. 'I'm worried about Lucy and the sooner we leave the better.'

Her voice was calm, unhurried, unlike his heart as he struggled for an equal composure. 'I've fuelled the truck and packed emergency supplies,' he said. She nodded but still wouldn't meet his eyes again and suddenly it was impossible to continue until she did. 'Kate?'

'What?'

How could she keep talking to the wall?

'Look at me.'

Finally she did, chin up, her beautiful grey eyes staring straight into his with a guarded challenge that dared him to try and break through her barriers. There was no doubt he'd love to do that. But he knew he had no right to even try.

In that brief moment when she looked at him he saw something behind her eyes, something that hinted about places in her that were even more vulnerable than the delicate young princess he'd left behind, or maybe he was imagining it.

Either way, he wouldn't delve because he wanted to close doors on this trip, not open them. 'For the next twelve hours I'll drive, you care for your patient and I'll get you both to Derby safely.' Then he'd say his piece and leave. 'So we'll talk on the way back.'

She blinked and he could sense the loosening of the tension in the air around her. Sense it with what? How could he sense things like that about a woman he'd not seen since they were both teenagers and yet not be able to sense anything about others more recent? It wasn't logical.

'Of course.' Her glance collided with his for a long, slow moment before she looked at the clock. 'Thank you, Rory.'

When she turned away, Rory swore he could feel physical pain from that loss of eye contact like tape ripping off his face. There you go. He still had it bad and, to make it worse, he doubted she felt anything. But that was his problem, not hers. He looked through the door to the patient on the bed. They needed to go.

To Kate's relief, Rory had them ready to leave within minutes and she couldn't think of anything else she might need to take with her. Except maybe her brain.

The grey matter seemed to have slowed to about one tenth speed since Rory McIver had walked in and Kate found her eyes drawn repeatedly to his easy movements as he settled Lucy in the back with extra pillows. He didn't look at Kate again, which was good, because Lord knew what expression she had on her face.

Her friend Sophie had come in to man the clinic. 'Don't worry if you don't get back for a couple of days. We'll be fine.' Sophie hugged Kate.

A couple of days with Rory? Kate shuddered. She'd never survive.

Sophie was still talking. 'I'll ring the housekeeper about your dad while you're away and drive up to the home station after work if needed. Okay?' Sophie frowned and Kate knew she could see the worry on her face. 'Just go.'

Kate nodded again and cast one anguished look at Sophie. Kate was the only midwife. She had to go.

She focused on her patient. Lucy's blood pressure had settled marginally with the antihypertensives and Kate had packed as many emergency items as she could think of, including what she could for the birth. Kate just prayed she wouldn't need any of it.

Even better, Rory had spoken to Lucy and her mum and by the time he'd shut the rear door to the truck Lucy was looking more relaxed, which was a good thing. Kate doubted it was all to do with the drugs she'd been loaded with and a lot to do with the handsome man promising to get them through.

As much as Kate dreaded the trip with Rory, she could only be secretly thankful that he'd been here. Otherwise, with Charlie gone, she'd be embarking on this dash with the elderly mechanic due for his own retirement soon. Old Bob would have been little help in a real emergency, with his flaring arthritis and his hearing aid that never worked.

The driver's door opened and Rory climbed

in behind the wheel—all six feet four of him—and Kate had to shake her head at her preposterous predictions this morning. So much for expecting Rory to be unfit from too many late night doughnuts and morose from his work; there was no doubt this guy was still seriously gorgeous, with a wicked twinkle a long way from surly.

Suddenly Kate was glad she had to stay in the back with Lucy because Rory's broad shoulders seemed to stretch halfway across the seat in the front and no doubt she would have been clinging to the passenger door to avoid brushing against him.

When he turned his head for one last check to see they were settled, his teeth showed white like a damn toothpaste commercial, Kate thought sourly, when he smiled at their patient. He didn't smile at Kate. 'You ready for your Kimberley Grand Tour, Lucy?'

The bronzed muscles in his neck tightened and his strong arms corded as he twisted, and Kate couldn't help the flare in her stomach or the illicit pleasure of just looking for a long slow heartbeat at this man from her past. No wonder she hadn't been able to forget him.

What she had forgotten was how aware she'd always been of Rory's presence and now, unfortunately, he'd hardened into a lean and lethal heartbreaker of a man who'd be even harder to forget. She wished he'd never come back.

She sank into her seat, glad of the dimness in the back to hide her momentary weakness, but even there she could pick up the faint teasing scent of some expensive aftershave, something the Rory she'd known would never have owned. The cologne slid insidiously past her defences and unconsciously she leaned forward again to try to identify the notes.

He looked at Kate. 'Did you get a chance—'

he frowned at the startled look on her face and hesitated, then went on '—to let them know at the homestead you'd be away?'

The slow motion ballet of his mouth as he spoke ridiculously entranced her and, after another of those prolonged thumps from her chest, her hearing finally caught up. She blinked as his words registered. Stupid weakness.

'Yes.' That'd been a staccato answer so she softened the one word with a quick explanation in case he thought her unnecessarily terse. 'I said I'd be at least a day late coming back, if not two. They'll tell my father.'

She looked away from him and decided then and there that it would be best if she didn't look directly at the source of her weakness again. *Don't look at Rory.*

Her teeth nibbled at dry lips as she pondered her worst fear out loud. 'That would be as long as we don't get more rain and end up flooded somewhere along the track for a night.'

The road they were about to hit was known as the last great driving adventure in Australia. It was enough of an adventure just being on it with Rory, let alone if they got caught up in the middle of a flood.

He nodded. 'It's a possibility. Let me know if you want me to stop more often so you can check Lucy out. I don't expect to get much speed up or you'll both be thrown all over the truck.'

He turned back to face the front. 'We'll drive until after the first major crossing…' he paused as if he was going to say something but then went on as if he'd changed his mind '…and stretch our legs.' He started the engine.

'Sounds fine.' But all she could think of was how much she wanted to get going so this agonising exposure to Rory could be over with.

Kate checked Lucy's stretcher safety belt,

forced a smile for her sleepy patient and buckled her own belt. She'd take it one hour at a time and not think about that talk she'd have to have on the way home. But it was hard when she had to decide what and how much to tell him.

Maybe she could leave him in Derby and drive the truck back herself. The idea had merit but, unless Rory had changed more than she expected, he'd be unwilling to send her off on her own.

The wind whipped the scrubby grass and stunted gums at the side of the road as they drove towards the distant ochre ranges and lifted the red dust they stirred into the now grey-black sky behind them.

At least the wind would shift the dust cloud more quickly when the road trains drove past, Kate mused, and, as if conjured, Rory slowed their vehicle and pulled close to the edge of the road to widen the distance between them and an oncoming mammoth truck.

The unsealed road was an important transport access for the huge cattle stations that lay between the infrequent dots of civilisation.

Road trains were three and four trailer cattle trucks that thundered backward and forward across vast distances. These road monsters didn't have a chance of stopping if you pulled out in front of them.

Even overtaking a road train going in the same direction was difficult because the dust they stirred was so thick that visibility was never clear enough to ensure there wasn't other traffic heading your way, and the risk far outweighed the advantages.

Kate remembered pulling over and brewing a cuppa instead of following one heading towards Derby in the past. She was thankful this one was travelling in the opposite direction.

This truck sported a huge red bull bar that flashed past Kate's opposite window and three steel-sided pens filled with tawny cattle rattled after it. She sighed with relief when the dust was blown away by the ever-building wind and they could move on.

An hour and a half of corrugations later, they came to the first of the major rivers they'd have to cross, the Pentecost. There was barely any water over the road, a mere eighteen inches, but that would change as soon as the storm hit. Then they'd be stuck on the other side until it went down.

Kate caught a glimpse of a silver splash from the bank ten metres back from the road and shivered.

Thank goodness the height of water was easy to see because Kate had no desire to watch Rory walk the Pentecost to check the level.

Not that anyone walked across here. The Pentecost was populated with wildlife and a saltwater croc might just decide it fancied a roll with him. The name saltwater crocodile didn't mean these creatures needed to be near the sea. They were quite happy to eat you a couple of hundred kilometres inland in freshwater. Even with her dread of the 'talk', that wasn't how she wanted to avoid Rory's company.

Rory slowed the truck for the descent into the river bed, changed into low range and then chugged into washed gravel to crawl though the wide expanse of water. Once across, they steadily climbed out the other side until back on the road and trails of water followed them as the truck shed the water they'd collected.

She looked up front through the windshield to where they'd stop. Her stomach dropped. Not here!

Ten years ago, Rory and Kate had set up a picnic at sunset out here to enjoy the glory of the Pentecost River and the distant ranges. That night before Rory left he'd wanted a place that wasn't her father's land and this was where they'd come. A point on the triangle of vast distances people thought nothing of travelling.

The memory was etched indelibly and Kate felt the soft whoosh of time as she remembered. That sunset had been as deeply coloured as a ripe peach with the magnificent sandstone escarpment of the Cockburn Range in the distance. She blushed red-ripe herself at that memory because that evening she'd set out to seduce the diffident Rory and they'd both got more than they'd bargained for.

That was their round-bellied boab up ahead. She just hoped Rory would have more delicacy than to pull in there.

The truck slowed and turned off the road into the lay-by. She glanced around for an alternative. Trouble was, theirs was the only decent sized parking area clear of the road and their boab was part of it. She sighed.

Grow up, she admonished herself. She needed to check Lucy's blood pressure and her baby's heart rate but the memories of this place all those years ago crowded her mind as she waited for Rory to open the door.

Kate remembered the night before Rory left ten years ago and unfortunately it was as clear as yesterday.

'So you are leaving?' Kate couldn't believe it. Rory gone? What would she do without Rory? He stood tall and lean and somehow distant, as if he had to be aloof to say what he needed. This wasn't her Rory.

Safe in his arms was the one place she felt loved for herself. He was the one person who understood how lonely she'd been since her mother had died, the person who could make her laugh at life and made her complete.

'I'm leaving tomorrow morning. With the

cattle on the road train,' he said and the words fell like stones against her ears. How would she bear it? How could he?

He went on, 'I can start my paramedic degree in two weeks. I have that. When I asked to marry you we both knew he'd fire me.'

He paused and looked away from her and she knew it was to hide his shame. He had nothing to be ashamed of. Kate wanted to hug the memories away from him. She knew what had happened. She'd overheard her father flay the pride from Rory as if he was a criminal.

She'd tried not to listen to the threats and abuse but if her father had thought she would think less of Rory from that exhibition then he was wrong. She was ashamed that she had Lyle Onslow's blood in her own veins.

'I'm sorry for my father, Rory.'

His eyes stared at the distant hills with a determination she'd never seen before. 'It doesn't matter.' He reached into his pocket. 'I have something for you.' He snapped open the box. 'Will you wear this until I come back?' he said, and pulled the ring free. She recognised it as a tiny pink diamond from the mines behind Jabiru—a token she had no idea how he'd managed to pay for—and slid it on her finger, where it sat, winking prettily at both of them. No matter that her father had refused permission.

She looked at the ring—Rory's ring—it could have been the largest diamond in the world and it wouldn't have been any more precious, but most of all she wanted to comfort Rory. Apologise for her father, show him how much she loved him. All she could do was pull Rory's face down to hers and kiss him. They were alone under the vastness that would soon turn to night. Their last night together.

'I want to marry you. I do,' she said. For the first time she dared to gently ease the tip of her

tongue into his mouth, awkwardly but with all her heart and soul in that one timid adventure, and suddenly they had entered a whole new dimension that sent spears of heat flicking from her through to Rory.

He groaned and kissed her back, answering her challenge, each emboldened by the other, enticed by the danger until both were mindless with the desperation his leaving had ignited between them.

She needed to feel his skin, hear his heart and she fumbled open his shirt and slid her hands against his solid warmth, up and down, not really sure what she should do but needing to feel and mould the hard planes of his chest—a chest she wouldn't have near to lean on if he went.

She could feel the shudder in his body as he sucked in the air he needed for control, groaned with what she did to him, and she rested her hand over his heart and soaked in the pounding of his life force.

That was when she realised she had power. She could move him and make him lose a little of that tightly leashed control he'd always had. Push him to the edge and maybe he'd take her with him over to a place they'd always pulled back from.

He tried to put her away from him but she wouldn't let him, flung herself back against him, pulling his hands up to caress her in return. Then it changed; she wasn't the one in charge.

Suddenly she was in his arms, carried to the blanket she'd set up for their picnic, laid gently on the grass and he was beside her.

'Are you sure?' His whisper over her ear.

'Yes.' No second thought. 'Kiss me.'

Then they were unbuttoning, discovering the places they'd left secret, venturing with her murmurs of pleasure and encouragement to seal their pact once they'd fumbled with their inexpert attempt at protection.

Kate realised she had her hand on her throat and the pulse beneath her fingers rushed with memories. The truck had stopped and she dragged her thoughts back to the present with a shiver.

They'd be gone from here soon and so would the memories that clung to her in this place like entangling cobwebs. She'd only need a minute or two to check Lucy and hear what she couldn't as they rattled over the corrugations.

Still sleepy, Lucy stirred and opened her eyes. 'Where are we?'

Kate laid her hand on her arm. 'It's okay. Pentecost River. How're you feeling?'

Lucy blinked like an owl. 'I can hardly keep my eyes open.'

'It's the drugs for your blood pressure. Just

doze as you can. I need to listen to your baby and check your observations while we're stopped.'

Lucy nodded sleepily and Kate slipped her stethoscope into her ears to listen for Lucy's blood pressure. All the while she was aware that Rory was walking around the truck towards the rear doors and any minute now she'd have to face him. That wasn't going to be as easy as it should be with those intimate memories so vivid in her mind.

Lucy slipped back under her sheet when Kate had finished.

Rory arrived, opened the back doors and waited to hear the verdict. 'Lucy okay?' His bulk blocked some of the light that spilled in with the open air and Kate was glad of the dimness because the heat had rushed into her cheeks and, uncomfortably, into other places too.

She licked dry lips. 'Better. Blood pressure's one forty on ninety. Much improved. I'm happy if it's still sitting at ninety diastolic.' Kate eased her cramped knee and sighed. She'd have to get out and stretch. It was crazy not to walk around the vehicle to move her legs for a minute before they set off again. She just hoped he'd move and she wouldn't have to squeeze past him.

As if he read her mind, he stepped away and, once out, it was hard to stifle the urge to catch a glimpse and see if their initials were still engraved on that tree.

She looked away to the river and realised Rory had moved up beside her, not touching but watching her. That was the worst thing. He didn't have to touch her—she could feel his aura and there was nothing she could do about the tide of heat that again ran up her neck. Or the aching desire to just lift her hand and rest it on his cheek. Where had everything gone so wrong between them?

'Our initials are still there, on the tree,' he said.

Kate's heart thumped at him reading her so easily. She was twenty-six, for goodness' sake, too old to be self-conscious about adolescent romanticisms. It would be horribly awkward if he saw how weak she was.

She stepped past and thankfully her breathing became easier. Away from him.

Rory didn't know what to say. The memories were there for him, bombarded him here, and he hated the way she threw an offhand glance at the tree. As if it meant nothing.

'We were vandals,' she said, and he winced at the unexpected pain her comment caused. 'You'd get fined for that nowadays.'

She was so cold, Rory thought, and more like her father than he'd ever thought.

She pointed to the river, no doubt to change the subject. 'I stitched up a traveller two weeks ago from down there.' They both looked. 'The croc only nicked his fingers when he bent down to fill his water bottle.'

Rory whistled through his teeth. 'Now that's one lucky man.'

Kate smiled grimly. 'Tell me about it.'

No. He wanted her to tell him about what had happened ten years ago. Why she'd changed so dramatically. Why she'd broken her promise and said she didn't love him. Sent the ring back.

Had her father made her? Had Rory's own parents had something to do with it? Now there was only Kate to ask.

Why had Lyle Onslow victimised Rory's father? Why fire him for no reason, stop his mother working anywhere on the station until they'd had to leave? Had the old man really been so afraid that Kate could love someone socially inferior like Rory?

Rory opened his mouth and then closed it. He

sighed. 'I'll top up the diesel with the jerrycans while it's not raining.' He walked away.

It wasn't what he'd been going to say. Kate knew that. That was the problem. They'd always had an intuition about what the other was thinking and it seemed she hadn't lost hers either. She gazed out over the plains with the serpentine swathe of the river and the thick dark clouds almost obscuring the base of the ranges they'd watched that evening.

The day she'd become a woman. A day that would affect her for ever. And Rory didn't know. Would he understand? Would he hate her? Blame her? Feel sorry for her?

'You right to go?'

'Absolutely ready to go,' she said, and they both knew that was exactly what she was thinking.

Lucy had dropped into an uneasy doze and didn't wake when the truck started again. Kate watched her patient's flushed cheeks and a tiny niggle of fresh worry teased at her brain, pushing away thoughts of Rory.

'It was a beautiful sunset that day.' Rory's voice was quiet and she knew it wasn't only the sunset he was saying had been beautiful for them.

Not now. Not with the memories so fresh in her mind. She felt the tears sting and she waited for them to form but of course it didn't happen. She couldn't go there.

Thinking about that time of her life would open up all the wounds and grief and anger she'd bottled up for so long and she wasn't sure what would ensue if she let them out. She was used to being frozen now. It was safe.

Her glance rested on the young girl opposite her. With Lucy so sick, now was the time to be focused on her patient.

'I don't remember.' She met his eyes briefly in the mirror and shrugged before she busied herself with writing down Lucy's observations.

Rory didn't comment but, strangely, not once in the next hour did she feel his glance in the mirror as she had since Jabiru Township.

When Lucy moaned softly in her sleep Kate narrowed her gaze on the bulge of Lucy's stomach. She eased her hand down to gently rest on the top of Lucy's uterus through the sheet. As she'd suspected, Lucy's belly was firm and contracted beneath her fingers but, thankfully, after only seconds, the tightness loosened and her uterus relaxed.

It was probably a Braxton Hicks contraction and not the real thing, Kate reassured herself, but the fact that Lucy had felt it even when half asleep was a worry.

Kate glanced at her watch to note the exact time. She hoped Lucy didn't take up regular moaning because then she'd have to start thinking the unthinkable.

Please. She didn't want a premature baby

born hours away from hospital in the back of an ambulance truck.

Closer to Derby might be okay. For about half an hour even the tiniest babies usually managed with warmth from the mum, and she could offer oxygen, but longer than that they had a tendency to crash. The risks increased dramatically for breathing difficulties, let alone all the other things that could go wrong.

She'd never enjoyed her stints in the special care nursery, no doubt because it had been too close to her own skeletons in the closet, and she knew premature babies became ill from lots of things. She knew that sometimes they didn't make it.

Like hers. Like the child she'd never even seen, for all those reasons she'd never been given, and the memories she didn't have that she'd blocked out successfully until now, until Rory had returned and allowed them to crowd her mind again.

Kate chewed her lip. 'How long do you think the trip's going to take?' She had a fair idea of the answer; she just needed to ask it out loud and to share the anxiety that was building as she jammed the untimely images from the past back into their hidden cave.

'Five hundred kilometres to go, at say fifty an hour is ten hours plus stops and moments of unusual interest. We've done two.' Rory looked up for the first time in a long time and caught her eye in the rear-vision mirror. 'I can shorten it by an hour but the ride will be rougher. Getting nervous, Kate?'

Understatement. Not about the labour—just the baby. 'Maybe we should have stayed at the clinic and had Lucy's baby there. At least we'd have electricity and more hands.'

'But they said ship her out.'

'I know. The problem is there's a real risk if Lucy's blood pressure continues to climb.'

FIONA McARTHUR   67

Not to mention the haemorrhage risk, Kate thought, but didn't say it out loud in case Lucy woke up. Already placental vessels would be damaged and weakening from the constant high pressure of blood. If one of the vessels burst it would pour blood between the placenta and the uterus, then mother and baby would be in big trouble. Like Kate had been. She'd have to watch Lucy for pain that didn't come and go.

'I think she's starting to contract,' she said quietly to Rory. 'Still irregularly, but the Nifedipine doesn't seem to be holding her.'

Rory frowned. 'Are you saying nature wants that baby out and she might go into labour?'

'Most likely. I'm all for that.' Kate grimaced. 'Just not on the road.'

Rory looked up at her again through the mirror and, while his face remained serious, his sincerity shone through. 'That's why you're with her. I've got faith in you. And I bet Lucy does too. Everything will be fine.'

It was a platitude. An attempt to ease her strain. He was a very experienced paramedic and ambulance officer, a professional at calming people in stressful and extreme situations.

And it was the phrase he'd said to her many times over the years in her hours of need.

That first day at school... As the boss's daughter, she'd been left alone and lonely until big Rory McIver from Year Two took her hand and showed her where she could sit. 'Everything will be fine,' he said and something in his eyes and the caring tone of his voice allowed her to believe him.

That week her mother and stillborn baby brother died... When everyone else avoided her, not knowing what to say. When her father banned her from a final farewell at the funeral and Rory sought her out and held her and helped her make a special garden with a wooden cross where she would go to talk to her mother that no one else knew about. 'Everything will be fine,' he said.

Rory, listening the hundreds of times she was upset by her father's uncompromising stand on her behaviour and mixing with the hired help. He was always able to reassure her. Big things became manageable when she told Rory.

Now here he was, doing it again. The funny thing was, while she knew it was a platitude, his words and the memories of the past times he'd said it did make her feel better. He was right. Worrying would achieve nothing; she would do the right things and be prepared as best she could. Now he was doing it again and she wondered if he realised. She couldn't help the warmth of her smile because it was tied in with so many good memories she shared with him.

'Thanks, Rory.'

She saw his surprise, shock even, because she'd been sincere in her gratitude. Kate thought about that. For the first time she began to wonder how Rory felt about seeing her after all this time. She wasn't the only one who had memories. It put a whole new complexion on her behaviour towards him and didn't help her to keep her distance.

This wasn't good. She couldn't go there, begin impossible dreams or resurrect old emotions that could overwhelm her. She hastily shut the thoughts down.

'You're welcome,' he said, but this time he kept his eyes on the road and she was glad!

A short while later Lucy moaned again and

Kate glanced at her watch before sliding her hand down to confirm the contraction. Fifteen minutes since the last one.

CHAPTER THREE

Rory so wanted to ease the lines of worry above Kate's eyes, smooth her brow and tell her again that everything would be fine, but she was the expert here and she wouldn't thank him for further interference.

Why he'd imagined he'd need to put himself through this torment when it was plain she didn't give a hoot about him, except to be vaguely irritated by his presence, he had no idea.

Had he needed to come back here and get it rubbed in his face in person? Hadn't the letter been enough? And the return of his ring? He must be a masochist. She'd told him ten years ago she didn't love him any more.

He just needed to get this trip over, Lucy to safety, and he'd never see Kate Onslow again. It wasn't as if Jabiru Station was anywhere near his normal world now.

He'd pulled himself up from nothing in his profession, had been promoted almost every year without pause until he was one step away from the top job. He had no need to feel like the hired hand he'd been ten years ago. It seemed he couldn't remove the stigma her father had left him with until he was an unqualified success. Until he had the one job that proved he was the best.

His appointment as Deputy Commissioner came into place in a week. After the closest battle between him and a more experienced officer, a family man who a lot of people said should have got the job, but the board had chosen wonder kid Rory because he'd promised them one hundred and ten per cent commitment.

Then, inexplicably, he'd wavered after reading an article saying that Kate's father was sick, and suddenly he'd needed to finish what lay between them. He'd promised the service he'd be back. He wished he'd never left Perth. Had turned back.

'I'm wondering if we should turn back.' Kate's voice intruded, almost as if she'd said out loud what he'd been thinking.

She was talking to herself and he didn't know whether to offer an opinion or not. Then she said something he hadn't expected. 'Rory? Have you ever seen a baby born?'

He dragged his mind away from his regrets and considered her question. 'Of course. And read the textbooks.'

She nodded but he could see she wanted more. 'When?' she asked.

'Last year. Just a couple of city babies in a hurry. All I had to do was catch and keep warm till hospital. But it's your area and your call, Kate.'

Rory remembered the cries of the woman, the fear in her face and the imploring way those eyes had begged him to relieve her pain. Apart from the methoxy' for her to breathe, there hadn't been a lot he could do except hold her hand. No, he wasn't comfortable with it but he'd cope.

Rory divided his concentration between negotiating the potholes and corrugations of the dirt track and Kate's face in the mirror. He had nothing helpful to add. She knew better than he the limitations distance imposed on keeping Lucy and her tiny baby safe.

She chewed those full lips of hers and he dragged his eyes back to the road. He remembered when he'd first noticed she did that. Always when she was worried. It had been when they'd started dating. And he'd kiss her to make her stop.

'It's hard to call it,' she said, and he concentrated on the red dust in front, anything to drag his eyes away from the damage she was causing. It seemed she needed to sound out her concerns and he was fine to listen.

'If we go back to Jabiru Township and Lucy doesn't go into proper labour until tomorrow or the next day, then I've placed her baby at a disadvantage.' She shook her head. 'This baby should be born at a level three nursery at least because, prem or starved, it will need watching.'

'No one said your job was easy, Kate.'

He heard her sigh. 'In an ideal world I'd like an ambulance with neonatal staff to meet us somewhere halfway if she goes into labour. I'm no expert on sick babies. I'm a birthing girl.'

He could hear the extra tension in her voice as she wondered out loud. 'Maybe they could fly in and meet us at one of the bigger stations, perhaps?'

He thought about it. 'Maybe.' But he knew she wasn't finished.

'This is Lucy's first baby—surely we'd have enough time for that?' She sounded more sure.

To Rory that seemed sensible. 'We could phone them.'

'How?' She shook her head and he saw again the depth of her concern. 'There's no phone coverage out here, unless you have a magic callbox in your pocket.'

He pulled his satellite phone from the glove compartment and waved it so she could see it. 'Boys toys. One of the perks of my job.'

She glared at him and it was queer how even that was endearing. 'How disgusting that you have a satellite phone in the city,' she said, 'and the clinic doesn't have one out here where the need is real.'

Technically, it wasn't a perk. He'd paid for it himself so he could be reached anywhere for his job. And she didn't need to know that he could easily afford it, but he made a mental note to anonymously donate one to Jabiru Township when he got back to Perth.

'Do you want me to connect you now and you can talk?'

She shook her head and he suspected she might even be a little ashamed of her outburst. 'I'll wait. Now that I know we can get advice I can sit until Lucy definitely goes into labour.'

'No problem.'

Her relief gave him an insight into the responsibilities of someone in her and Sophie's job at Jabiru. Like a road ambulance crew, they'd have to make the hard decisions too, without the backup of a nearby hospital, manage emergencies and manage the same horrific injuries he did, but on their own until help could arrive, sometimes many hours or even days later.

At other times they'd need to encourage people to leave their homes and families and travel huge distances for their own safety, at sometimes great expense as well, and occasionally the worst wouldn't happen. It made him realise his Kate was a big girl now.

Half an hour later Kate stared unseeingly as Lucy breathed in and out in her sleep and allowed her mind to drift until, unexpectedly, Rory slowed the truck and prepared to stop.

Kate peered through the windscreen to what lay ahead. At the side of the road a small but sprightly white-haired lady waved them down from behind her camper van. She wrung her hands together as she waited for them to pull up and Kate's stomach tightened. Not a mechanical breakdown, then?

The lady leaned in the front window as Rory pulled on the handbrake and Kate could see the glitter of tears on her wrinkled cheeks. Kate closed her eyes in dread.

'You're in an ambulance?' The little woman sighed and shook her head. 'Too late. How ironic.'

Kate was glad she wasn't driving without Rory because he was out of his seat and beside the woman before Kate realised his door was open. She blinked and tried to work out how he'd done it. She guessed that was what ambos did all the time. Quick on the scene, quick to prioritise and assess, she'd never really appreciated that before. Rory would be very good at it.

'How can I help you?' Kate could hear the gentleness in Rory's voice and, despite the woman's suggestion that there was little they could do, he didn't waste time until he confirmed it. He steered the woman back to her compact little van.

'My husband.' Kate could hear her careful enunciation, as if she spoke slowly the words would finally make sense. 'I was driving. John went to sleep the last time we stopped. He said he was tired. But I didn't know he'd never wake up again. He's cold now. I didn't even say goodbye.'

'Can you show me?' Rory said, still in that gentle, caring voice that brought tears to Kate's own cheeks, and she could just hear him murmuring sympathy as he went to confirm there was nothing they could do.

Kate glanced at Lucy, thankfully still asleep, and she hoped she wouldn't wake if Kate climbed through to the front and out of the passenger door in case Rory or the new widow needed support.

Kate glanced at the empty road around them and tried to imagine what the lady had been thinking before they'd pulled up.

It wasn't a common occurrence on the track but she'd heard of tragedies like this before and she wondered if her husband would have been happy to go like this. What type of sad courage would it take for his wife to drive all the way home to an empty house, wherever home was?

Kate chewed her lip and followed their stark footprints in the dust. She avoided looking at the van until the last moment and, when she did, she saw that it had a picture of a gaily painted wagon and the words 'John and Jessie's Jaunt' written on the back.

She winced as Rory and Jessie climbed back outside.

'There's nothing you could have done. He looks very peaceful,' Rory said, and he rested his arm around the woman's shoulder as he drew her towards Kate. 'This is Kate. She's from the Hospital Clinic up at Jabiru Township.'

Jessie glanced at Kate and bit her lip as she tried not to cry. 'Hello, Kate.'

'Hello. Jessie, is it?' Kate pointed to the painted names. 'I'm so sorry. We can phone the

Kununurra police station and they'll meet you here as soon as they can.'

Jessie looked back at Rory. 'Thank you, both of you, for your kindness but I'll drive to the next town myself. They can meet me on the way. I've lived with this man all my life. I can drive now he's gone to the next.' She gave a watery smile. 'He'll be watching from above for the way I change the gears.'

Kate didn't know what to say. 'You do whatever feels right. Did you have any warning? Was your husband well?' She wanted to leave Jessie with an opening if she needed to talk.

'I thought he was.' Jessie choked back a sob. 'But he was in remission, and we've been having a wonderful time before the next set of treatment.'

'It must be very hard for you,' Kate said.

Jessie nodded and drew a deep breath. 'At least I don't have to watch him die slowly and painfully at home. When I get over the shock

I'm sure his going will be a blessing.' Her eyes filled. 'But I will so miss him. Fifty years and he still made me laugh.'

Rory and Kate looked at each other over Jessie's head. Imagine a relationship like that! It seemed they were both thinking the same thing. As one they looked towards the van. How could they leave her alone with the body? 'We'll stay till the police get here,' Rory said.

Jessie thought about it. 'No. Thank you. I'll be fine.'

Kate moved closer and slid her arm around Jessie so the widow was supported by both of them. 'If we do go on, we'll wait until you feel ready to drive. Would you like me to make you a cup of tea before we leave? I've a Thermos in the back I filled this morning.'

Jessie sniffed. 'That would be nice.' She lifted her chin. 'And don't you worry about me. There's nothing for me to be afraid of. I'll just say my goodbyes as we drive and the children will organise the rest when I call them.'

Rory used his phone for the police at Kununurra and he and Kate stayed for another ten minutes until Jessie drove off on her final journey with her husband.

'She's very brave,' Rory said. 'He looked a kind old gentleman.'

'I'm glad. It's almost fitting to drive the last drive with just the two of them.'

Rory watched the van disappear. 'Would you do that?'

Kate looked away. 'I'll never be in that position.'

Kate sat in the back as the scenery flashed past. They passed another dust-swirling road train full of cattle and crossed two creeks but not much was said. No doubt Rory was as busy with his thoughts as she was with hers.

If she and Rory had still been together, they would be in their tenth year. So much time wasted wanting the impossible and she should have been looking for someone like John to share her life with. Before it was too late. But it was too late. She was too scarred for any man.

Jessie had children to help carry the load and Kate had a gaping void where hers should have been.

'What's wrong, Kate?' Rory's intrusion into her thoughts only made it worse.

'Nothing. Nothing you can help with.' Kate sighed. It wasn't Rory's fault. He'd been a brick to drive her to Derby and she hadn't really thanked him. In fact, she'd been hard on him and was lucky he was as even-tempered as he was.

She still didn't know what he'd come back for, except to see her. She didn't know how she felt about that, apart from terrified he'd break down the wall she'd hidden behind for so long. But he was right. There were things that needed to be said between them.

It was almost with relief that she heard Lucy moan because that put paid to worrying about either of them.

Lucy's eyes flickered open and she pushed her hand down onto her stomach. 'It hurts, Kate.'

Kate sat forward, even as her heart rate accelerated. A constant pain would be a dangerous sign. 'Where does it hurt, Lucy?'

'In here—' Lucy rubbed her stomach down low '—and in my back. It comes and goes.'

Kate was relieved. Labour was not optimum, but for a horrible moment she'd thought Kate was going to complain of severe headache or liver pain, or the signs of concealed haemorrhage—all ominous signs of internal damage from her hypertension.

Lucy screwed her face up and her eyes sought Kate's. 'What's happening?'

'I think you're going into labour, Luce.' She squeezed the young girl's hand and Lucy clung to Kate's fingers. 'Why don't you sit up straighter and get the weight off your back and side for a while?'

Lucy struggled into an upright position with Kate's help, which wasn't as tricky as it could have been because for the moment Rory had picked up speed and they flew along a freshly graded stretch of the road without the usual corrugations.

Lucy instinctively sighed a big breath out and her shoulders slumped; even her fingers loosened on Kate's. 'The pain's going now.' Her eyes sought Kate's and her voice wobbled. 'I'm starting to get scared. What if my baby is born out here on the road?'

Kate looked into Lucy's eyes and willed her to take in Kate's own faith in a woman's ability to give birth. Something her midwifery had thankfully reinstilled in her. Kate did believe that. Every woman's body had it—except Kate's, that was—but she wasn't going there.

She spoke slowly so Lucy could absorb the message. 'Your baby will be tough like his or her mother. Like you are. Have faith in your body, Lucy. Labour can take a long time and you'll know if you're getting closer to the pointy end. We can't do much about how your labour is going to work out here, just trust it, because everyone is different.'

Lucy nodded, so Kate went on. 'Go with it, ride the waves and relax, and think of your little baby waiting to meet you.'

Lucy searched Kate's face and must have seen the conviction there because she finally nodded. 'Okay. I can do that.'

Kate sat back and smiled, proud of her young patient's willingness to trust her own instincts—and Kate. 'I'm here and so is Rory. In a while we're going to ring the hospital in Derby and see if they can meet us somewhere if you get into strong labour. We'll look after you and your baby, no matter what.' Her eyes drifted to Rory's in the mirror. He was watching.

'Do you want me to stop so you can check her out?' he said.

Kate shook her head. 'How long to the next stop?'

He glanced at his watch. 'Half an hour to the general store. You could use the landline there too, talk to Derby; might be easier to hear if the satellite reception is playing up.'

Past the point of no return, then. At least Kate knew there was no turning back. 'We'll be fine till then, thanks. I'm just glad the real rain held off for this long.'

She smiled down at Lucy. 'You'll be able to get out, go to the Ladies and stretch your legs.'

Not long later a flash of lightning ahead and

the almost immediate crack of thunder warned them they were heading into the thick of a storm.

Suddenly the heavens opened and the road ahead turned the previously smooth dirt into a sucking quagmire. As the heavy sheets of rain flooded the mud it made visibility and stability tough. Rory cursed silently under his breath and he glared skywards. If it had held off a little bit longer it would have been good.

His hands tightened on the wheel as he felt the truck slew sideways and he accelerated briefly until the off-road tyres caught and he had traction back. 'Might take a little longer,' he called over his shoulder and slowed down until the truck was barely making a brisk walking speed and they ground their way towards the hills through the middle of the storm.

'I'm glad I'm not flying in this,' he heard Kate say to Lucy.

'Me, too.' Lucy's voice wobbled and Rory

looked out of the side window and winced as a flash of light illuminated the sparse scrub. He could agree with that but it wasn't much fun driving either. He was just glad that he was the one carrying such precious cargo because the retired Charlie had been night blind ten years ago and Bob was even worse.

A little over three-quarters of an hour later they pulled up at the rustic roadside store that marked the half-way point of their journey and Rory was able to pull up under cover to let them out.

They stayed just long enough to achieve what they had to. Kate rang Derby to update them and promised to phone at the next stop, if not before. Rory topped up the diesel and bought takeaway coffee for all of them to go with the sandwiches they'd brought, while Lucy slipped off to the Ladies.

He had a few minutes to quiz Kate, at least. She looked strained and he didn't doubt she was feeling the weight of her decision. 'So how do you think she'll go?'

Kate chewed her lip at him over the rim of her paper cup and for once there wasn't any of that reserve he'd felt between them since he'd come back. Somehow, that was even harder to bear.

She seemed to shake off her preoccupation while he waited and he wondered for a second if he was making this easier or harder for her by being the one to drive them to Derby. Then he mocked himself for even dreaming his presence made a difference.

Kate seemed to have come to peace with her decision. 'If Lucy labours and progresses to birth then we'll just do the best we can. I think she'll be fine. We'll be fine. If that's the way it goes, then we'll concentrate on the quickest way to get the baby to the special care nursery in Derby.'

So there was a chance they'd have the baby in the truck. Rory's brain froze for a second. Lord help them. That was definitely not what he'd expected her to say.

'Do you think that's going to happen?'

Babies. He knew next to nothing, really. Give him a ten car pile-up any day. He knew what to do with massive trauma and advanced life support. He knew how to coordinate disasters, reallocate staff, vehicles and modes of transport. But the idea of a premature baby—he remembered those pink and shiny, almost see-though miniature babes from air ambulance trips—relying even a little bit on him was more scary than he'd bargained for.

Kate looked serene now and Rory felt like shaking his head. She continued with, 'I'd say there's at least a fifty-fifty chance of her progressing to birth, especially now she's in early labour; it just depends.' He closed his eyes.

Oblivious, Kate went on, 'Of course, if she breaks her waters then I'll up it to eighty percent.'

He tried to keep his voice level. 'You seem pretty calm about it.'

'Not a lot we can do about it now.' Kate smiled at him. 'Who's the person who says everything's going to be fine? I can see you're not comfortable.'

Rory rubbed the back of his neck uneasily. 'Women should have babies in hospitals, where it's safe.' Not in the back of rough old ambulance trucks in tropical storms on a dirt road miles from civilisation.

'There's many that would disagree with you, including most of the Aboriginal women around here, but we'll save that argument for another day.' She obviously didn't think they were totally out of their depth so he'd just have to trust her.

He thought about her word choice. So she'd

argue with him another day? Suddenly it wasn't so bad and he smiled at her. 'I'll hold you to that discussion at a later date.' And Kate would be there to do the baby stuff.

When Rory bundled them back into the truck for the next stage of the journey the rain had eased but still fell in soaking sheets.

'How do you feel after that walk around, Lucy?' Kate put away the BP machine. 'Your blood pressure's good.' Kate thought Lucy looked less sleepy, but she wasn't sure that was a good thing.

'Okay—' Lucy's voice dropped to a whisper '—but maybe I didn't go to the toilet enough 'cause I think I've just wet myself.'

O-oh. Ruptured membranes, Kate thought as she lowered her voice. 'Little wet or big wet?'

Lucy blushed and hung her head. 'Medium.'

Kate chewed her lip. Okay, then. 'You could have a little tear in your bag of waters around baby, Luce.' Kate dug into one of the emergency bags she'd brought. 'See if you can slide this feminine pad into your underwear. I know it looks like a big white surfboard but it'll make you feel more comfortable. As a bonus, we'll be able to tell if the dampness is from the water from around the baby and how much is coming away.'

When Lucy had accomplished that feat, not easy in a swaying vehicle, Kate pulled out the tiny Doppler to listen to Lucy's baby. The steady clop, clop, clop of Lucy's baby's heartbeat could be just heard over the rain on the roof.

So baby didn't mind someone pulling the plug out of the bath, she thought. They were all silent for a minute as they listened, that just discernible galloping heartbeat a reminder of why they were driving through the ridiculous weather to Derby.

'Should be about two hours to the next diesel stop,' Rory said when Kate put the Doppler away. 'Then, not long after that, the road will improve as we hit the main highway.'

'So we'll get through all right?' Lucy's voice was hard to distinguish over the rain and Kate repeated the question to Rory in case he hadn't heard.

'They said at the shop the next causeway hasn't risen too much with the downpour yet,' he said.

Kate hoped he was right but she wasn't so sure about the return trip for her and Rory. Not much they could do about that except worry later and see.

When they reached the next crossing the water had risen to a little over eighteen inches but the causeway was concreted and the vehicle high. The truck drove through smoothly without any water coming in the doors.

Kate was glad now they'd stayed only briefly at the last stop.

The rain eased more as they drove towards

the next mountain range they couldn't see, she knew it was there, but today it was well and truly hidden in cloud. She mentally shrugged. If they kept going they'd find it eventually.

CHAPTER FOUR

'THE pains are getting stronger.' Lucy's forehead was wrinkled with the effort to breathe slowly and calmly and Kate smoothed out her own frown as she watched.

'I know, sweetheart.' Kate glanced up and caught Rory's eyes in the mirror again for a fleeting second, just for her own comfort, before she looked back at Lucy. 'Keep your breathing going, you're doing beautifully. It looks like this baby of yours is pretty keen on seeing what the world looks like on the outside of your tummy.'

Lucy grimaced. 'I think I just wet myself again. This time it's a flood.' She shuddered in disgust.

Kate smiled. 'Okay. We might get Rory to

pull over for a minute while we sort out what's happening down there.' She looked to the front of the vehicle as they slowed. There was no doubt Rory was on antenna duty and could hear most of what they were saying, which saved her having to repeat everything.

There was nowhere sheltered to pull in so Rory edged to the side of the road as much as he could without sinking into the soft mud. The last thing they needed was to be run over by a road train or bogged in wet bull dust mire and have to dig themselves out. Neither was a great option.

Rory had caught snatches of conversation for the last half hour and had an idea things had progressed in Lucy's labour. They were still an hour out from the next stop but he'd been thinking along the lines of pulling off the track and down one of the side roads because they were 'near' one of the larger cattle stations.

A detour of maybe fifty kilometres would see

them at a place that had facilities and an airstrip for when the sky cleared.

Kate pulled the privacy curtain while she attended to Lucy and Rory reached for a map from the seat beside him to see exactly where they were. The last crossing had been about sixty kilometres back so that made them near the turn off to Rainbow's End Station.

It wasn't a tourist facility like the high-end Xanadu they'd passed two hours ago, but he remembered the McRoberts family from the camel races when he was a kid. They'd certainly have no problem in an emergency like this.

But maybe it was quicker to keep rolling towards Derby and meet up with the ambulance coming the other way. He'd see what Kate wanted as soon as she was ready to tell him what was going on.

'Rory! I need you.' A calm voice but with that hint of urgency that had him jerk aside the curtain and heave himself in beside Kate without any hesitation.

He glanced at Lucy and blinked. The girl's whole body shuddered as the seizure took control and her half closed eyes stared vacantly at some point over Kate's left shoulder as her body shook the stretcher in jerking movements.

Rory slipped the oxygen mask over her face as Lucy's skin paled to alabaster. During the fit her body would use up the oxygen faster than she breathed it in and the tinge of blue around her lips deepened. Rory could feel his own heart gallop like the baby's heart rate had through the Doppler earlier.

Kate was focused and in control, which boded well for Lucy. Rory glanced at Lucy's stomach, which seemed to be heaving with a life of its own, and his fear for her baby mounted. He was so glad he wasn't the only person here.

'It's okay, Lucy,' Kate repeated. 'It's nearly over. We're here with you. It's okay.' Kate's soft voice repeated the litany until, after what seemed an hour but was probably less than two minutes, Lucy's body slowly settled and then lay still.

A deep dragging breath from Lucy was echoed by the one Rory pulled in for himself as he glanced at Kate before he wiped Lucy's face. He knew about fits. He'd dealt with epilepsy often but not with a pregnant woman and all he could think about was the lack of oxygen for Lucy's baby.

'The first eclamptic fit,' Kate said as she reached for the medication roll. He didn't like the sound of that.

'You expecting more?' He hoped she'd say no but of course it was likely. She handed him an ampoule and syringe and Rory busied himself with drawing up the medication while Kate checked Lucy's blood pressure.

'Her blood pressure's shot up. And we'll probably have to put some Magnesium Sulphate up in a drip to lower her cerebral irritability as well.' Kate reached into another side pocket and removed an intravenous fluid flask to add drugs for slow infusion. 'But we'll start with more hydralazine for her blood pressure. After you draw up I'll grab that satellite phone of yours, please.'

They worked seamlessly. Rory prepared the drugs, Kate checked and then injected them. Rory loaded the flask. He'd work with her on the road ambulance any day. No fluster or indecision—just how he liked it, his partner calm and the patient prioritised efficiently. She made everything easy, which was usually his job.

It was strange to remember that this was his Kate. The young woman he'd known years ago would have looked to him to save her. That time had certainly passed. He didn't know how he felt about that but there'd be time to think about it later.

'I thought her blood pressure was down.' Rory looked at Lucy who, while still pale, breathed normally now.

Kate sighed and nodded as she rechecked the blood pressure on Lucy's arm. 'So did I. Obviously not enough for Lucy's seizure threshold. Some people seize with an almost normal blood pressure, just like some babies can have febrile convulsions with only low temperatures.' She shrugged. 'If that's how their make-up is. Lucy's mother fitted. Either way, we need help.'

But what collateral damage? Rory thought. 'And her baby?'

Kate spared him an understanding glance. 'Will be fine. So far. The oxygen supply to the uterus was only decreased for a minute or two. As long as Lucy doesn't have long fits or do something nasty like separate her placenta with a haemorrhage, the baby will rest like Lucy and then recover. Babies are designed to take some stress.'

He knew he looked unconvinced as Kate elaborated. 'Lucy's out for the count but her labour will probably progress more rapidly now.'

Rory winced down at his chart, where he recorded the drugs and time given. 'More excitement to come, then.'

Kate flashed a smile back at him. 'After this, I'll be much happier when this baby is out.'

Happy? He was far from that. 'As long as one of us is happy.'

Lucy moaned and shifted her head from side to side but still didn't open her eyes.

Kate frowned and ran her hand over Lucy's abdomen. 'I'm not *that* happy.' She bent closer to Lucy's ear. 'Your uterus is contracting strongly now, Lucy. That's what the pain is. Soon.'

'Do you want me to head to Rainbow's End Station? It's less than an hour away. At least we'd have facilities and an airstrip.'

Kate had the Doppler out to check the baby's heartbeat. The clop, clop was marginally slower and very regular but Kate couldn't hear any slowing after the contractions. She stared at him for a moment and then nodded. 'I'll check with Derby but that sounds great. Let's do it.'

Rory nodded and he could hear the baby's heartbeat follow him as he climbed back through to the front, where he grabbed the satellite phone and passed it back before he started the engine.

Kate's voice echoed around his head. This Kate was a new woman, so much more independent and bolshy than the one he'd loved with every ounce of his adolescent heart and she seemed quite capable of handling any situation. She certainly didn't need him.

Kate, the person who had given his life

meaning all those years ago, then had taken it away on a whim, leaving him a driven man. It amazed him to see her so gentle and calm as she talked to the semi-conscious girl and he was just as affected. Even though she was not part of his future, he could still feel proud of the woman she'd become.

Kate loosened her shoulders and took her own deep breath. Well, that was the first fit out of the way. Thank goodness Rory had been here. She'd have hated to try and cope with Charlie or Bob at the wheel.

Hopefully, Lucy wouldn't have any more fits before the drugs kicked in. 'It's okay, Lucy.' Kate stroked the girl's arm. 'You'll start to feel better when baby's born and the placenta that's causing all this trouble has gone.'

She checked Lucy's BP again and then picked up the phone. Lucy moaned and Kate slipped her other hand down to feel the contraction at the top of Lucy's uterus. 'Your baby's fine and looks like he or she is determined to come soon.'

Kate dialled the number for Derby that she'd kept since the last stop. As she waited to be transferred through to the obstetrician on call she peered out of the window. 'Is it my imagination or is the sky becoming lighter?'

Rory started to answer but Kate said, 'I hope so,' before he could. He remembered she'd had a habit of that. The memory drew an unwilling smile.

'The storm seems to be concentrated more over the way we've come,' he said quietly, then stopped as she lifted her head when they answered.

'Hello? Yes, Doctor, it's Kate Onslow again.' She waited. Then, 'Lucy's just had one eclamptic episode lasting two minutes and her BP's now one sixty over a hundred.'

She listened. 'Foetal heart rate one hundred and fifteen,' and then nodded her head. 'We've given the Hydralazine. Start the Magnesium Sulphate? Sure. I've got the protocol. No problem.' She looked across at Rory and he waved the prepared flask.

'She's in established labour and we'd like to divert to Rainbow's End Station for the birth.' She paused, then, 'About an hour. We'd wait there until RFDS can come and get them both. How's the weather at your end?'

She smiled and Rory smiled too. It lifted his spirits to see that Kate again. So, good weather report, he gathered.

'Our weather isn't quite that here yet, but good news. So you'll ring Rainbow's End and tell them we're coming. Great. We'll see the plane there, then. Thanks.'

Kate put the phone down on the ledge and took the loaded flask from Rory and this time she gave him the full-blown grin that he'd give his brand new, fully equipped, supercharged Range Rover for. 'We work pretty well together, don't we?'

'Funny, that,' he said dryly. Maybe that's because we should have been together ten years ago, he thought with a tinge of bitterness. 'The weather's clearing and I'm guessing they'll get back to us with an arrival time?'

She nodded and turned to speak softly into Lucy's ear. 'Rory's going to take us to Rainbow's End Station and we'll wait for the plane. Just rest as much as you can, Lucy.'

The track to Rainbow's End seemed to take forever but he doubted Kate would have noticed. Things were hotting up in the back.

Lucy began to moan every few minutes and Rory realised his own shoulders had begun to tense just before the next contraction was due.

'You okay, Rory?' Kate moved up near his

seat for a moment and he had the almost irresistible urge to reach back for her hand. A bit of personal comfort wouldn't have gone astray.

Instead, he said, 'I think you have enough to worry about apart from me, Kate.'

'Just to let you know, when Lucy moans it's because she's listening to her body, not because she wants us to do anything.'

He could feel himself frown. 'You're telling me she's not in pain?'

To his surprise, there was even a smile in her voice. 'Oh, it hurts all right. I'm telling you she's not scared of the pain. So don't feel you're failing her by not taking it away. Her own body is dealing with the pain by releasing endorphins. If it was overwhelming her it would be different. Okay?'

'Okay.' He didn't understand but he had to believe Kate. And, now he thought about it, Lucy didn't sound frantic or in a panic. She sounded almost drugged already. 'Thanks, Kate. It was bothering me she was upset.'

He felt her hand lightly on his shoulder and then she was gone. He only just heard her quiet, 'Thought so,' as she sat back down again next to Lucy.

The rest of the drive didn't seem as bad. Rory sighed once to relieve the tension in his shoulders and focused his concentration on the conditions.

Soon he barely heard Lucy because the road was half covered by water in places and it was his job to get them to the station without mishap.

Finally the lights of the homestead could be seen on the hill ahead. Lucy had become more agitated in the last five minutes and Rory had begun to doubt Kate's pain theory.

'Stop here, Rory!' That quiet yet immediate voice again from Kate.

Rory pulled over and by the time he stopped he could hear the sound he'd heard twice before in the back of an ambulance—the sound of a mother easing her child out into the world. And he could hear Kate's voice as he climbed through.

'Beautiful, Lucy. Nice and slow. Just breathe your baby out with the pains and relax between.'

'What do you need?' Rory whispered as he looked around, but it seemed Kate had everything ready.

'Just that towel when I ask for it. We'll dry baby before laying him or her on Lucy's skin, and if you check Lucy's BP as soon as it's over that would be great.'

'Baby on her skin?'

Kate's voice was barely audible and he had the feeling she didn't want to distract Lucy from her thoughts. 'Lucy's a natural born heater. Best place for a newborn is on mother's chest.'

He'd been thinking airways and resuscitation. Wrapping in space blankets. Apparently, that was out too for newborns. He leant over and spoke into Kate's ear. 'Breathing-wise?'

Kate shook her head and frowned but she glanced at the neonatal bag and mask she had ready. 'The heart rate is great. There's no reason to think baby won't be fine. You always give them thirty seconds if the heart rate's good before you interfere. If smaller than I expect, I'll wrap his or her body up without drying in that roll of cling wrap there, and then onto Lucy's skin to keep warm. Just dry the head and pop that little cap on.'

'Cling wrap? Plastic sandwich wrap?'

He saw the flash of her teeth. 'Neat, eh? Little babies get really cold from draughts and thin plastic wrap keeps air off wet skin. When the team arrives, if they want to access an arm or leg they just make a hole in the wrap for that part of the body. Keeps baby insulated.'

'We have all the mod cons in this ambulance.'

'Actually, I brought it with me but feel free to add it to your list when you go back.'

When you go back! The words were like a bucket of ice over the warmth he'd been feeling as he shared this moment with Kate and Lucy. He shook the thought off but some of the excitement had been diluted by reality.

'It's coming,' Lucy said on an exhaled breath and Rory stopped talking. He saw Lucy's hand clenching on the sheet and he slipped his hand over hers. She grabbed his fingers gratefully and he cursed himself for not thinking of it sooner.

'You're doing a great job, Lucy,' he whispered in her ear and squeezed her hand back gently.

Kate was down the business end. 'Here comes baby, Lucy. Nice and slow.' There was a pause and then the rest of the head appeared, then, strangely, baby's face turned as if to look the other way. Rory looked up at Kate with a question.

'Restitution,' she said quietly. 'Untwisting of the neck that happens as the head is born. Baby's head is lining back up with the shoulders.'

Then, gracefully, one pale shoulder appeared and seemed to take a dive towards the bed and then the other was out and in a rush it was all over as hips and knees and feet all tumbled into Kate's waiting hands. Kate held up the baby so Lucy could see the sex of her baby.

They all waited for the first indrawn breath or cry. The little girl lay limp and still like a stunned fish in Kate's hands, dark blue eyes wide open in a tiny unmoving face—no cry, no breath.

Kate froze. Time stopped. Her breath jammed and her heart dived sickeningly in her chest to beat one slow beat after another. It was as if she'd fallen, unsuspecting, into a freezing black shaft filled with ghouls. Down and down and down into a bottomless hell. The seconds ticked with aching slowness as the shock battered her. Dead like her baby! Lucy's baby couldn't be…

'Kate?' Rory's voice shocked her back to the real world and she looked at him and then shook her head to rid it of the panic. The world sped up.

'I'm sorry.' She sucked in a breath. Lucy's baby would be fine. It was just blue and stunned. 'Towel,' she said to Rory. She even sounded calm as she rubbed the flaccid baby until it began to gasp and flex in protest.

Oblivious to those seconds of Kate's frozen moment of horror, Lucy reached down to touch her baby. 'A little girl.' Tears ran down Lucy's face. 'A shame my mum wasn't here to see.' Then she reached for her daughter and Kate passed the towel back to Rory and slipped the little girl up to her mother.

'There you go, Lucy.' Lucy closed her arms over Missy.

Kate looked at Rory and their eyes met over

the new mother and her baby. She could tell Rory was euphoric at the birth, and the fact that he'd shared it with her. She just needed a hug.

She didn't even want to think about what might have happened if he hadn't been here. How long would she have stayed frozen?

'This is the needle I spoke about to help separate the placenta, Lucy.' Kate slid the needle in Lucy's thigh but Lucy didn't seem to notice, then Rory watched Kate clamp and cut the cord.

He wanted to hug Kate. All these things she had to remember. He murmured a saying he'd once heard. 'The midwife, methodical through the beginning of life.'

Rory was back in that warm place of sharing; his throat felt tight from emotion and he looked at Kate and then Lucy with wonder, and maybe even a tear in his eye. 'You are amazing, Lucy. Congratulations on your beautiful daughter.' He pumped the blood pressure cuff up as he spoke.

'Thank you.' Lucy smiled up at him shyly. 'And thanks for holding my hand.'

'My privilege.' Rory watched the meter as he let the cuff down and winced at the height of Lucy's blood pressure. 'One eighty on one ten.' He shifted back out of the way.

Kate nodded and tucked the blankets around mother and baby so that Kate's daughter was chest to chest with her mother's skin and her little head was bonneted and turned to face Kate. 'I expected that. I'll give another dose of Hydralazine now the placenta is delivered.' She smiled a wooden smile at Lucy. 'The good news is your daughter looks great. She's tiny, probably about four pounds, but perfect. She was just a little stunned at birth and will be looking for a real feed because she's smaller than she should be. I think she's not too prem, just very hungry from the placenta shutting down. See, her ears are perfectly formed.'

Kate took the Hydralazine from Rory and slowly injected it into Lucy's second drip line.

When she'd finished, Rory gave her the saline flush to clear the line, then said, 'I'll get us up to the house,' and he crawled back through to the front of the vehicle.

Within seconds they were making their way up the driveway. All the lights were on and the door flew open as they arrived.

The next half hour blurred as Lucy was transferred from the vehicle to a comfortable bed. Mrs McRoberts had been a theatre sister before her marriage and she insisted that Kate and Rory relax after their adventures for 'five minutes at least' with a cup of tea while she watched Lucy and her baby.

It had been a stressful couple of hours and Rory was happy to take advantage of the offer. He wasn't sure about Kate, who was circling the table as if she couldn't bear to sit down.

She stopped with her back to him and faced the paddocks.

Rory hesitated and then crossed to stand behind her. When he touched her shoulder she flinched so violently his hand flew up in the air. 'Hey,' he said and deliberately put both his hands firmly onto her shoulders and eased her back against his body. 'Take a couple of those deep breaths you keep recommending everyone else takes.'

To his relief, she did, her shoulders rising and falling beneath his hands. After an initial stiffness, she relaxed enough to lean into him a little, then inexplicably she pulled away and sat down. Rory let his hands fall through the empty air and turned to look at her where she sat.

He didn't get this woman at all—which would be fine if it didn't feel as if he'd just been kicked in the gut every time she shut him out—so he shrugged and sat down himself.

When she spoke it was as if nothing had happened between them and Rory decided to drink his tea. He had to find a way to stop her messing with his head.

'Apparently, after the storm left here it seems to have headed Jabiru way,' she said. 'No chance they'll have planes landing on the strip there.' The way she avoided his eyes and spoke reminded him of this morning, before they'd left, and he felt as if he were riding a roller coaster of emotions. One minute she was fine, the next she'd retreated so far he could barely see the real Kate.

She poured more tea and then glanced at her watch. 'Mrs McRoberts said the plane's only half an hour away from here. We can head back after that.'

Something was going on and he had no idea where her thoughts were. He watched her face. 'So you're not going to go with Lucy to Derby?'

She shook her head. 'No. She's had her baby now, and they're both fine.' She shut her mouth with a snap and he almost missed the moment when she started to shake with reaction. The shudders grew until her whole body shook the chair. Almost like Lucy's fit, only with such anguish on her face he could no more not go to her than not breathe.

Rory pushed his chair out and dropped to the ground to kneel beside her chair. He pulled her head down onto his chest and held her. 'It's okay, baby. Everything's fine. You did wonderfully.'

She stared straight through him and for a moment a horrifying feeling hit him that he'd lost her to some place he couldn't go.

'Kate? Honey? You okay?' She didn't move and he tilted her chin and looked into her face. Eyes tightly shut, she leaned into him and her arms crept round his chest, drawing comfort as if she couldn't help herself. They sat like that, him rocking her, for what seemed to Rory like forever.

After a few minutes she sighed and sucked in a shuddering breath before she rested her forehead against his chest. When she leaned back her eyes opened and she blinked at him. She glanced away and then back. 'I'm sorry. I don't know why I did that. Thank you.'

He smiled and brushed her cheek with his finger before he sat back on his heels. Ignored her deliberate distance as if it wasn't there. 'You're welcome. It's been a pretty big day.' He brushed the hair away from her eyes so he could see her face. 'You okay now?'

She drew another erratic breath. 'When the baby was born…' Kate shook her head at the memory. 'I had a brain freeze. I thought the baby was going to die. I've never done anything like that before in my life.'

He stroked her hair. 'I didn't see that. It

must have been quick because we didn't notice. I thought you were just waiting for the baby to breathe by herself. It was only seconds until you dried her.'

She frowned. 'I shouldn't be here. It's all been too much.'

'You've had a lot of responsibility with Lucy.'

'Not just Lucy.' She shook her head again. 'My father, you coming back…' she paused '…and the past.' She shook her head. 'I don't want to talk about it. I can't.' He watched her emotions shut off from him like a roller door closing until there was nothing. No connection at all.

The last thing he wanted to do was upset her again. 'Fine.' He stood up and moved back to his chair as if he'd done something mundane like picking a napkin off the floor. He moved the topic on to what he hoped was safer ground. 'So Lucy will go on from here without us?'

He watched Kate sit back in her chair and

compose herself more. She took a sip of tea, a couple of breaths and even offered a false smile before she nodded. 'The flight nurses are excellent and her aunt's at the other end. Her aunt will stay with her until Mary can come. I need to get back to town and eventually back to Jabiru Station and my father.'

Rory didn't want to think about Kate's father, what the man had done to his parents, and his own issues with him. Or what he'd done to Kate to have her wound up like this. The return part of the trip would be hard going enough without broaching the subject of Lyle Onslow. Not yet. Maybe never.

He scouted for a safer topic. 'Lucy's daughter is a cute baby. Missy's a cute name. What do you reckon she weighs?'

Kate looked away towards the room where Lucy lay cosseted by Mrs McRoberts and she smiled for real this time. 'Nearly four and a half pounds on the kitchen scales. She looks almost term, good creases on her feet and hands. So her tiny size is because she's been having it harsh in there with Lucy's blood pressure. Hypertension plays havoc with transfer of food and oxygen from the placenta. Our baby's got a bit of catch-up feeding to do.'

The expression made him smile. 'Our baby. I like the sound of that.' Rory repeated the words without thinking but he was unprepared for the absolute devastation in Kate's face.

He could only blink in disbelief as Kate pushed her chair out and turned away. 'I've got to go.'

'Kate? What's wrong?'

'Nothing. Leave it.' He could hear the anguish in her voice and Rory felt the waves of despair radiating from her as she put her hand up to ward off any questions. She hurried away to Lucy and he stood and stared after her as his brain tried scenarios to explain what had just happened.

He looked back at the table with the two half-finished cups and he shook his head. His eyes narrowed. He didn't understand but he would. Later, when the plane had gone.

He picked up the cups and headed through to the kitchen to thank the housekeeper. The rain had stopped. He'd tidy the truck and refuel and when the RFDS arrived he and Kate would run Lucy out to the airstrip and say goodbye. Then all this would be settled.

CHAPTER FIVE

THIS was exactly why she'd known seeing Rory was a bad idea. Not once since that dreadful morning when they'd said her child had died had she spoken about her loss.

Ten years ago she'd been confused, isolated from anyone she knew and told to pretend it had all been a bad dream. She'd spent the next six weeks physically healing and mentally bricking up what had happened behind an impenetrable barrier.

Until Rory. The one person she couldn't hide from.

How was she going to get through the return trip? He was going to ask, in that caring, genuine way of his, about something he more than anyone had the right to ask. Did she have the right not to tell him?

Kate felt like throwing herself off the veranda and running into the hills so that Rory wouldn't find her but of course she couldn't. No wonder she'd decided emotions were better left out of the equation and her life.

The time for her to be alone with Rory drew closer and the tension inside her built until she was sure she'd explode. Finally, Rory and Kate stood together beside the truck out on the dirt airstrip. They waved to Lucy as she was loaded onto the small aircraft with her baby for the flight.

Her eyes slid sideways as Rory shaded his eyes to watch the door close. Shame Rory hadn't taken that plane back to Derby, Kate thought. Then she wouldn't have to go through this. 'You should have gone with them, Rory.

You could have made connections and been in Perth tonight.'

They watched the RFDS taxi off down the runway under the heavy sky and Kate chewed her lip as she wished she'd decided to go with Lucy.

'That would defeat the purpose of my trip.' Rory looked at her. 'Wouldn't it?' He frowned. 'Have you forgotten why I'm here?'

As if she could. 'I'm quite able to drive the truck back myself.'

Rory examined her lovely but stubborn profile as she watched the plane. 'I'm sure you could manage the truck beautifully. But it's not happening.' He turned away. 'It's later than we anticipated. Do you want to stay here the night or leave now?'

His gut instinct said to stay the night here and not risk the trip back to Jabiru on the slim off chance they'd get through but he knew Kate wanted to get home. Either way, he planned to get her alone and find out what it was that had changed her from the young woman he'd left behind ten years ago.

Still she didn't look at him. 'My patient's gone. I'd prefer to leave now but it's your call.'

He sighed. 'It's after four. It would be very late if we did make Jabiru tonight. But if we leave tomorrow to cross the larger rivers there's less chance the crossings will be passable at all.'

'Then leave now.' Still that monotone from Kate that had him frowning down at her.

'I think we should freshen up as long as we're quick. They've offered late lunch and a hamper for the road. It seems sensible to take advantage of the hospitality.'

'You can't do both, Rory. Make up your mind.'

'Sure we can. We'll eat quick and I've already fuelled the truck.'

Kate looked through him. 'You've decided, then. Why ask me?'

He shook his head. Women. She'd changed since that incident earlier. Her face looked drawn and closed and he could barely picture her smiling in the back of the truck during the drive.

It was a battle he wasn't going to win at this moment. The RFDS plane was in the air now. 'Let's go, then.'

They were on the road within half an hour and Rory picked up the speed a bit because he had no patient to be bounced around in the back and Kate safely beside him in the front.

She hadn't spoken a word since she'd buckled her seat belt and he had things to think about too. Like why she'd had such a crisis and been angry with him when he'd done nothing that he could see to cause her displeasure. He took a stab in the dark, which seemed appropriate because the sky had suddenly become grey with threatened rain.

'Have you had a bad experience with a

patient's baby in the past, Kate?' He glanced across at her and then back at the road. 'Is that why you were upset at the homestead?' It was all he could think of.

At first he thought she wasn't going to answer but grudgingly the words came at the same time as a gust of wind rocked the truck. 'You could say that.'

He tightened his hands on the wheel to keep the wheels in a straight line as he thought about her choice of words.

He knew all about bad cases at work. Emotional debris from other people's lives and disasters. Especially the good people it seemed to happen to. Maybe this was what'd changed her. He could understand that. 'Can you talk about it?'

She turned to look at him and he could see she'd erected a sheer wall like the steep-sided gorges that ran with water at the side of the road. The gorges had taken millions of years to form. He wondered how long that wall had taken to evolve in Kate.

She sighed and began, but her lack of expression was as eerie as the strange light they were driving through. 'The baby's mother had pregnancy induced hypertension the same as Lucy. Our dash with Lucy brought it all back to me.'

He nodded. 'I can understand that. Want to tell me about it?'

'No.' She stared at the road in front and he bit back a sigh. And waited. After a few minutes' silence he deliberately didn't break she did begin. 'They flew the mother out to Perth...' her voice trailed off '...but it was too late for the baby in the end. The placenta separated, she bled and the baby died.'

Rory could tell she needed to talk about it. He'd learnt that over the years in his job. The hard way. 'So did you go all the way with them? What happened to the mother?'

'Oh, I was there.' He thought for a moment she was going to cry and he had the urge to stop her from telling more. Protect her from the grief she'd bottled up, but maybe she'd never get over it if she didn't speak about it now.

Maybe he was the only person she could tell. His voice was only loud enough so she could hear over the wind. 'Go on if you can.'

'She was young like Lucy and quite sick for the next week. You know what they did? They never showed her the baby. By the time she was well enough to realise what had happened it was too late and she never saw her baby. They told her to forget it ever happened.'

'Monsters,' he muttered, and Kate nodded and he realised he must have said it out loud.

'You'd hate that happening to any patient,' he said and tried to imagine the ramifications for the young mother. 'No wonder you were upset.'

Kate nodded again and he saw the shine of

tears in her eyes before she turned away. He'd bet there was more. The case had obviously affected Kate heavily. He knew ambulance personnel who'd had a series of similar cases that built up inside and then one last bad one could paralyse with grief and regret.

'And that's why you agreed to transfer Lucy? Because you were scared that would happen again?'

'To make sure it didn't happen again.' She flicked a glance at him and he winced at the hunted expression in her eyes. 'I don't want to talk about it any more.'

He wasn't satisfied but backed off and then they rounded a corner and suddenly the world intruded again. It seemed it had a habit of doing that.

They nearly ploughed into a long-wheelbase luxury camper that had skidded and come to rest diagonally across the road in front of them. With their side of the road blocked and reluctant to brake too heavily in the greasy conditions, Rory aimed for the gap on the other side of the road.

He steered between the rock of the mountain they were circling, careered past the vehicle before he could slow the truck enough to stop without skidding, then pulled back onto their side of the road and slid to a halt.

He looked across at Kate to make sure she was safe and for the first time in a long time there was an animated expression on her face.

'Not bad, sir. Maybe I'm glad I'm not driving.'

'High praise indeed from you.' He grinned at her and she grinned back and the sudden rush of joy that blossomed inside him warned of danger and he tried to damp it down. Then the smile ran away from her face and he was sad to see it go because he'd felt as if they'd bonded briefly in that moment of relief.

Then again, that way lay pain and he'd have

to stop putting himself out there for the hits. He looked away to the camper. 'Let's see if they're okay.'

Kate slid from the truck onto the muddy roadside and it felt as if she'd just escaped from prison. She couldn't believe she'd started to talk about her loss, even if she'd hidden behind her fictitious patient.

The mire sucked at her boots as she crossed the road and she realised the driver of the van was knee-deep in mud behind the bus. The rear wheels were buried as he tried to manoeuvre what looked like plastic planks down to drive out over. His face was covered in smears and stripes of red slimy soil, as were most of his clothes. He didn't look too happy about it.

Kate mentally shrugged. He would have been more unhappy if they'd hit him. A little mud wouldn't kill him.

'I'm sorry,' the man said. 'I asked her to stand

at the corner and wave people down but she was too busy telling me how stupid I am.' He glared at the open door of the Winnebago before he looked back at them. 'I can't do anything with her.'

Kate turned to see a diminutive brunette, beautifully dressed and made-up, poke her head out of the door. The woman limped theatrically onto the top step with her red-tipped fingernails resting on her hips and waited for maximum effect before she stepped gingerly down another rung. Still safe above the layer of plebeian mud, she bestowed an overjoyed smile on Rory. 'Well, if it isn't Rory McIver.'

'Oh, Lord.' Kate heard Rory's muttered comment as she turned to look at him but his face was bland. He avoided Kate's unspoken question by looking at the other woman. 'Hello, Sybil,' he said.

Sybil's appearance was so incongruous—she

was dressed for a shopping expedition rather than a bush road trip—followed by Sybil's tone of voice when she'd addressed Rory, that Kate couldn't think of a thing to say. It shouldn't matter that Rory knew this woman or that he wasn't comfortable with meeting her here; what mattered was that some other vehicle didn't career around the corner and collect the lot of them.

Kate shook her head at the delay. 'We've hazard signs in the ambulance. I'll put them out on each corner and hopefully nobody else will have to steer for their life.'

With a narrow look at Rory, which confirmed that he actually seemed relieved she was going, Kate squelched her way in disgust to the rear of their vehicle and opened the back. Now who the heck was Sybil? And just how well did she know Rory McIver?

Kate ground her teeth. Well, what did she

expect? She hadn't seen him since he'd left Jabiru ten years ago and just because she'd been miserable didn't mean he had to be the same. As far as he was concerned, he hadn't lost a baby and had to claw himself back to sanity.

Rory watched Kate yank the signs from the back of the truck and sighed. He turned back to the job at hand. The sooner they were out of here the better, for lots of reasons.

'Why couldn't you be sensible like that lady?' the man said peevishly.

Sybil laughed. 'Don't be silly, Philip. Look at the cost. She's filthy like you already.'

Rory flicked a glance at Sybil before he made his way over to Philip. 'Watch it, Sybil. Kate and I can easily drive away and leave you.'

'But I need you to look at my ankle, and you wouldn't do that, Rory. I *know* you.' There was a world of meaning in her words and Rory couldn't help glancing to see if Kate had heard.

His heart sank when he saw her toss her hair as she stomped up the road with a sign. Yep. Explanations later, though.

Rory declined to answer Sybil and glanced at the dark sky. At least it had stopped raining for the moment. 'So what's your plan? Philip, is it? I'm Rory.' Rory held out his hand and Philip wiped his palm on a reasonably clean piece of shirt and shook Rory's hand ruefully.

'I was going to use these board things I found in the back. Apparently they're the best thing out for this, but if you've ideas I'm happy to listen. This whole trip—' he glared at the door Sybil had disappeared through '—was a bad idea.'

'Not your idea, I gather?'

'We're supposed to be going to the diamond mines. I wanted to fly but she wanted to drive through some town called Jabiru on the way. I was pretty happy up until an hour ago when she turned into a petulant witch.'

'That's Sybil for you.' Rory turned and measured with a glance the distance to the other side of the road and the logistics of the ambulance simply pulling them out. 'There isn't enough room for us to pull you forward, though if we slew sideways we might leave you worse off. Your vehicle's heavy.'

He rubbed the back of his neck as he thought. 'We'll winch you forward from one of the trees across the road; that's the safest. The problem is you'll be facing the wrong way when we finish. You'll have to turn around up the road if you want to come back this way.'

'I'm happy to head back to Derby and Broome. I don't suppose the road gets better this way?'

'Only worse with river crossings.'

'Let's do what you suggest.' Philip narrowed his eyes at the camper. 'She's not getting her pink diamond now, anyway.'

'If you'll take some advice, don't tell her that until Broome or your trip will be hell.'

Phillip laughed. 'You really do know her.'

Rory raised his eyebrows. 'I've paid my dues.'

Kate came back and helped with the reversing and soon the whole road was churned by their efforts. Kate could feel her tenuous hold on her temper begin to slip. At the edge of her vision Sybil limped dramatically on the dry side of the road as she tried to distract Rory. Everything seemed to be taking forever.

Kate didn't want a night beside the road with Rory, was terrified of it, in fact, yet the afternoon was slipping away.

Finally they managed to winch the vehicle free but by the time they were finished everyone, except Sybil, was covered in mud.

'Now can you look at my ankle, Rory?' Sybil's plaintive voice broke into the feeling of accomplishment the workers were finally savouring.

Kate turned her back so she didn't have to watch. She squashed down the ignoble voice that suggested she whisper to Rory not to wash his hands first. Why should she care about Rory looking after a woman from his past? She was glad he'd had a life. She should've had one herself.

Ten minutes later Rory and Kate were back on the road. 'How was poor Sybil's dreadful ankle?' Kate said and she didn't even care that her sarcasm made Rory raise his eyebrows.

'Only slightly swollen.'

'What a surprise.' Kate was steaming. 'And they've made us even later. It's almost dark.'

Rory wondered if her irritation was even a little out of proportion to the crime. The thought made him smile. 'We couldn't leave them stranded.'

Kate shook her head in disgust. 'She could have done something to help.'

'Some people are purely decorative. That's Sybil.' His sanity-saving mistake from the past.

Kate stared as if she didn't know him and she jammed one hand on her hip as she turned. 'How handy for decorative people. Wish I'd thought to be purely decorative.'

'You were pretty decorative ten years ago.'

She tossed her hair. 'I've changed, thank goodness.' She glared out of the front of the vehicle as they drove along. 'So where do you know her from?'

'Sybil? From Sydney, more than a few years ago. She helped me when I was having a bad time.' Like not long after I'd been dumped by you. 'I worked in a nightclub on my days off and she was going out with the owner. Then she looked me up again in Perth.'

'How nice for both of you. Spending quality time together. Well, it seems she was going to look you up in Jabiru. You must have made an impression on her.'

Knowing Sybil, she was much more devious than that, he thought. What would Kate think when he told her? There was a lot at stake here and she didn't see it. He'd been so in love with Kate he couldn't contemplate a relationship with another woman. Had told Sybil so. And, being a woman, she'd dragged a few details out of him. She'd always had a knack for re-membering the wrong things. What would Kate say? Especially as she seemed to have taken an instant dislike to the other woman.

'Actually, I think she was looking for you.'

Kate turned a startled face towards him. 'Why on earth would she do that?'

So Kate was still oblivious to the damage she'd caused him. It shouldn't hurt after all this time but it did. He'd meant so little to her. He really didn't want to have to spell it out.

He forced a smile and chose diversion in the ridiculous. 'You're not jealous, are you, Kate?'

Her lip practically curled. 'Spare me.'

He really did have to laugh at her disgust. He'd known she wasn't, of course, but no harm in wishing. He went on to explain. 'When I first met Sybil I may have used you as the excuse for not being married already.' To hell with it; he'd just say it. 'I said I'd left my heart in Jabiru. I didn't mention your name.'

He waited for her to comment on that, say she was sorry, even laugh at the idea, but she didn't say anything and he wasn't sure if that was good or bad so he concentrated on the road ahead and tried to forget he'd mentioned it.

After a few minutes when she still didn't offer any comment he looked across briefly at this militant woman who bore so little resemblance to the young girl he'd left ten years ago. Consciously he moved on from his own neediness. 'So what's your excuse?'

Now she looked at him. 'What do you mean?'

'Why aren't you married, Kate? Why are you still single and childless when obviously you were born to be a wife and mother?'

She didn't even look at him. 'I'm afraid that's none of your business.'

He could have ground his teeth in frustration. How could she say that? Rory turned to look at her profile. 'On the contrary, once it was very much my business.'

Unfortunately he'd had his eyes off the road far too long and when he glanced back he realised the evening shadows had hidden a muddy section deeply scored from previous vehicles.

He veered heavily to the left so that the ambulance swung towards the edge of the road and even climbed a little up the bank. For a moment he thought they were going to make it around the quagmire but the truck slid off the bank with a slurp, stabbed the thick tyre with a lethally pointed branch on the way and then the wheels inevitably slowed in the wet bull dust mire until the truck sank to the axles and stopped.

They wouldn't get out of this in a hurry. Bloody hell.

'Oh, that's great,' Kate said and crossed her arms with a pained sigh.

Strangely, her ill humour repaired his own. Actually, he'd done pretty well to avoid tipping the truck over. He looked at her for a moment and then said, 'Thrilled about it, myself. Looks like you've got my company longer than you anticipated.' Her behaviour reminded him of a much younger Kate and, despite her obvious irritation, the possibilities were in fact quite intriguing now he thought about it.

'Hmmph,' Kate said. 'You're just lucky you're not stuck here with Princess Sybil.'

'I'd much rather be here with you,' he said,

tongue stuck firmly in cheek. Kate glared at him and opened her door and he watched her jump down and stomp off.

CHAPTER SIX

Rory climbed out and surveyed their predicament, then started to whistle just to annoy her. He'd been in worse spots and the old Kate had never sulked long. That was another of the things he'd loved about her.

The road was a challenge but, well-equipped as they were, it would only take time. Something they didn't have much of before dark. He glanced around for a good place to camp.

A few minutes later Kate sidled up to him and she didn't quite meet his eyes. 'I'm sorry, Rory. I'm a cow.'

He grinned down at her. He remembered this Kate. Always brave enough to say when she'd been wrong. 'Well, Daisy,' he drawled—Daisy had been the house cow's name when they were kids—'we'd best winch our way out of this and set up camp back off the road. I'll change tyres in the morning.'

Kate smiled warily back and Rory felt the lightest he'd felt all day. Just one smile and she had him. He was as weak as water when it came to resisting Kate. Not much had changed.

They worked steadily for the next forty minutes as the light slipped away around them. Finally they'd extricated the truck and shifted onto higher ground on the bank so they wouldn't endanger any of the infrequent night travellers.

'You did well not to tip over when we hit the mud.' Kate shook her head as she watched him open the door to get out. She glanced at the offending wheel. 'And that's one flat tyre.'

Rory jumped down. 'Only on the bottom,'

he said facetiously and glanced around. 'I'll fix it tomorrow. Let's wash up and get the camp sorted.'

'I've set up a basin and the water bag on that log. If you want to wash I'll grab some wood for a fire.'

He raised his brows and looked her up and down. 'So you're not just decorative.'

She narrowed her eyes at him with the comparison to Sybil. 'You feel like living dangerously, McIver? Don't start me. And I'll have the stretcher in the back tonight in case it rains.' She raised her eyebrows at him. 'You can have it tomorrow night.'

He opened his eyes wide. 'Gee. Thanks. We'll be back in Jabiru by then.' She shrugged, unsympathetic, so he pretended to sigh. 'I'll guess I'll shake my swag out, then.'

She nodded and began to scoop up kindling and he watched her for a moment as she bent to pick up another twig. She seemed more settled since her mini-tantrum when they'd stopped. More relaxed and he didn't know why. But there was no doubt he was pleased to see it.

He glanced up at the sky; the clouds were breaking up a little for the moment. Hopefully, it wouldn't rain tonight.

Half an hour later they had the campfire set like a crackling little tepee in the middle of a clearing. Kate sat on the ground on top of Rory's swag with her knees drawn up and rested her back up against a blanket-covered log. Rory surveyed their campsite from where he leaned on a tree. They munched thick-cut cold beef sandwiches with homemade horseradish from Rainbow's End Station against a big fat boab tree.

'Mmm, mmm.' Kate couldn't remember when she'd last enjoyed food so much. The night air was cool, the fire crackled with orange flames and a few early stars twinkled in the gaps between the cloud cover now that it was dark. They were alone, the sky was enormous, and it brought back her deep love of the top end.

She glanced across at Rory; flashes of light from the fire illuminated the dark planes of his face. He was watching her. She realised he had been for a while and suddenly it wasn't so good they were alone.

She didn't want to talk about today and especially not about what had upset her. 'So tell me about your rapid rise to fame, Mr McIver. How does a country man like you make it so big in the cut-throat world of the city?'

Rory didn't say anything immediately and for a moment she thought he was going to demand they talk about her. The seconds stretched and the crickets and frogs seemed to turn up the volume of the night while she waited.

When he spoke she realised how tensely she'd waited and forced herself to relax.

'I decided early on that if I stayed in the Ambulance I'd have a big say in how things were run in the service.' He looked at her. 'So when I got your letter—' He paused, and Kate watched him look away from her and she had the first inklings of how deeply she'd wounded him.

He went on, 'I was gutted, couldn't get back to Jabiru to talk to you, couldn't get you on the phone, was trapped without holidays for another year and no money. I wrote letter after letter and when you didn't write back I pushed myself to succeed and didn't stop until I got there.'

So her father hadn't forwarded them on. She wasn't astonished, just sorry that she couldn't have made it easier for Rory. 'I didn't get any letters.'

'If you weren't there it's not surprising your father didn't forward them on.'

Kate remembered the day before he'd left

and the demoralising ridicule her father had heaped on him. She'd forgotten about that too, with all that had happened after Rory had left. Would it have made a difference in her choices if she'd remembered earlier—and more of the reasons why Rory had left?

'I'm sorry you were hurt. Go on.'

Rory brushed that away. 'Not much to tell. I worked non-stop, applied for every course. I took every overtime shift, every relief senior position offered, even if they were way out in the bush, while I did other correspondence courses.' He shrugged.

That amount of work wouldn't have left much time for play. In fact, it sounded a lot like her. She'd taken little time to enjoy her life as well. She looked away. 'As I said before, it sounds driven.'

'Guess I was.'

She looked up at him and shaded her eyes

from the brightness of the fire so she could see his face. 'So why are you here now?'

His voice dropped. 'Because I've come to a point where I need to clear what was between us before I can go any further.'

Kate balled the paper she'd unwrapped from her sandwiches and threw it in the fire. The silence between them stretched and she watched the flames curl around and blacken it until suddenly the paper burst into flame and was consumed. That was what would happen to her if she allowed Rory to expose her emotions.

'I'll ask again.' Rory's voice drifted from across the fire. 'Why aren't you married, Kate?'

She looked away and said the first thing that came into her mind. 'I never found the right man.'

She heard Rory suck his breath in. 'I was there.' He stood up and shifted until he loomed above her, staring down; she could feel his gaze without looking. Then he edged in beside her and moved along until his hip nudged hers. The heat from Rory's thigh against hers was even more flammable than the paper she'd just burned.

She reached forward for another stick and when she sat back she made sure there was a small gap between them; suddenly she could breathe again.

He frowned at her and moved his hip deliberately back against hers with a little bump, as if to say—this is where I'm staying. 'How can you say you never found him? I was there,' he said again.

'You left.' She didn't look at him but she felt his gaze boring into her. There was no escaping from this Rory. He was onto her and she'd the feeling he wouldn't be shut down like most people were when she put up her defences.

Rory sighed. 'I left for both of us. If only it were that simple.'

She shot him a glance and then her eyes skittered away. 'It was that simple.'

The walls, the walls, Rory thought, but at least

she was talking. They needed to thrash this out and clear the air so he could see the future. 'You wrote and said you didn't love me. Sent my ring back. Why was that?'

She turned her face. 'Things happened. I changed.'

What things? She was driving him insane. He shifted so he could more easily see her face. 'Do you have any idea what that letter did to me? I was studying my butt off, we'd been writing every week, then out of the blue you threw away our dreams.' He pulled his wallet from his shirt and opened the leather. 'This letter.'

He dug into the back section and eased it out. Faded and dog-eared, the yellowed paper lay in his hand accusingly, looking up at her.

He watched her put her hand out and touch it gingerly, and then she pulled her hand away. This was what he'd come back for. This answer. These reasons.

Rory sat back and tilted to face her again. His voice lowered until it was barely audible over the crackle of the fire. 'What happened, Kate? Tell me.'

She looked at him then and the same agony that had scared him at Rainbow's End Station was back in her eyes.

Rory ached to know what had affected her so deeply but he knew he had to go gently.

'I don't want to,' she said.

'Please, Kate.'

She dragged her hands through her hair and looked around with a tinge of desperation. He wanted to pull her into his arms and hold her tight to ease her pain, only he wasn't game to touch her in case he caused more damage or she jumped up and ran into the night.

Finally she began. 'Do you remember the night before you left, Rory?'

Rory nodded. He'd never forget it. He and

Kate under the old tree near the Pentecost after that horrific day. He'd had to drive somewhere off her father's property to talk. Couldn't say the things he had to under Lyle Onslow's starry roof. He'd been so young then.

He hardened his heart against the desolation in her face and dug the knife into the tree to finish '4 ever'.

'I'll come back.' He meant it with every breath because their love was as grand and magnificent as the vast Outback they'd both grown up in, but just as steeped in the tragedies of a harsh environment.

He loved his Kate so much it hurt and he'd die for her but at what cost to his future and that of his own family? He thought they had a chance if he went away.

'He fired me.' Rory shook his head at the sympathy he could see in her face. 'We knew he

would.' He didn't want her pity, just to get away and make a life for them, away from the poison of her father, so that one day he'd show him what Rory McIver was made of.

'Both our fathers told me never to speak to you again,' he said, 'but that's no surprise. Give me three years. I'll be back on my twenty-first birthday for you. After the first year I can finish the degree on the road so I'll save every cent for you. Wait for me. I'll be back. I promise.'

That was when he saw her realise he wouldn't change his mind and he jammed his hands against his sides to stop himself from reaching for her.

'Money isn't everything,' and she looked at him as if he'd stabbed her. 'Take me with you.'

He couldn't not touch her and cupped her chin so their eyes met and he could hold her gaze. Try to make her understand. 'I have to do this. You can't come with me until I have something I can offer. Something more than this.'

He pulled a ring from his pocket, a tiny pink diamond from the mines behind Jabiru, and slid it on her finger. No matter that her father had refused permission.

It had come in on the mail plane yesterday, cheap by her standards, and nothing like what he wanted to buy her, but he wanted that ring on her finger so at least it could be with her when he couldn't. 'Will you wear this until I come back?'

She was so young and he was sure that leaving was the right thing. 'It's because I love you I have to leave.' Kate Onslow had been the one person he could dream with and that dream included both of them.

Then she lifted her face and kissed him, and her sweetness and ardour and the thought of the months away from her helped drag him down under the tree and when she kissed him with a desperation he hadn't been prepared for things had got a little out of control. Actually, a lot out of control. 'Take me with you,' she said again.

In retrospect, he should have.

'I remember everything,' he said.

Kate lifted her head. Her beautiful eyes, filled with the darkest shadows from the past, stared into his. 'All right, Rory. Maybe it is time. But you asked for it.'

She stared at him for a long moment and then she said it, so quietly he almost didn't hear her, 'Seven months later I lost our baby.'

Rory blinked. 'What baby?'

She chewed her lip. 'Ours!' She glanced at him briefly to see if he understood and then away. 'Yours and mine. The one we made after our last night.'

He stared at her, unable to take it in. He'd

taken precautions, or thought he had, but it had been his first time too.

'The son I didn't tell anyone about, just like Lucy, until it was too late and I was too sick.'

Rory felt the shock hit him like a hammer in the gut. Kate had had a baby? First he was cold, then hot and then he stopped thinking about himself and the fruitless dreams that it would be too painful to think of right now, and thought of Kate.

His Kate had been pregnant at sixteen and he'd left her to face it on her own. With Lyle Onslow. Cold sweat beaded as he thought of how her father would have treated her. 'You should have told me.'

Her voice was flat. 'Father flew me out to Perth to a private convalescent hospital. I didn't know anyone and our baby was born by Caesarean section. Alone.'

The bastard. He dreaded the next question. 'The baby?'

She sighed. 'As I said before, I was very sick for a week and when I woke up it was too late. My baby was gone.' She turned stricken eyes to him. 'If I'd told my father earlier, maybe things would have been different but I was too much of a coward. My baby might have lived.'

Kate was the young girl she'd talked about. Not an unconnected case at all, but herself. Poor young, defenceless Kate and he hadn't been there. He tried to imagine the scenario. 'Who told you he'd died?'

'Some nurse. I'll never forget when that awful woman came in. She said it was just as well as I was so young. Earlier there'd been another, younger and kinder midwife, who'd said I could hold him but she didn't come back.' Her voice dropped even lower. 'She said she'd take a photo, a lock of hair and a handprint, but I think they stopped her.'

She drew a breath and went on more strongly,

'The awful one said he'd died from complications of prematurity and the separated placenta. I never even saw him.'

She looked at Rory with pure agony in her eyes. A devastation she'd carried bottled up for ten years. Rory wanted to kill someone for doing this to his Kate.

'I never saw who our baby looked like. What colour his hair was. The shape of his ears or hands—nothing.' She gazed into the fire. 'I think I could have borne it better if I'd said goodbye.'

Rory struggled with the monsterlike actions of a man who should have looked after her. 'Your father had no right to leave you to face that alone.'

She shrugged and rolled her shoulders to loosen the tension in her neck. 'For a long time I pleaded for information on what had happened. He kept saying, "Nothing happened. Forget it. There never was a baby."' She shook her head at the concept.

'By the time I'd left boarding school I was strong enough to stand up to him and I demanded the address of the funeral home. I even hoped faintly that the baby hadn't died, maybe he'd adopted him out, but I searched Perth, found Fairmont Gardens and there was a plaque. I'd found him. Baby of Kate Onslow. Lived for a day, and the date.'

Rory felt sick with self disgust. 'What date, Kate?'

She stared into the fire. 'The third of August. He'd been eight weeks premature and I'd never had a chance to name him.'

Rory looked at Kate and didn't know what to do—or say. She'd never forgive him for this. No wonder she hated him. 'I'm so sorry.'

'I don't blame you.' But her voice was flat and broken with memories and his heart ached for this woman who'd meant the world to him— still meant the world to him.

He tried to imagine what a young girl without a mother, or anyone to hug her, could do in the beginning to ease that pain. He guessed there wasn't much she could do without support except brick it up and try not to think about it. 'Did you go home at all?'

'No.' She shook her head vehemently. 'Why would I? I boarded in Perth and studied every minute to give myself choices. That's when I decided I'd stay for uni and do my midwifery. I'd be there for young mums.' She looked at him. 'This is the first time I've been back to Jabiru and you had to turn up.'

Rory couldn't grasp that she'd shut him out when she'd most needed him. 'It's been ten years. What about later? You never told me.'

She looked at him but there was no expression on her face. After what she'd just said. No expression. That scared him most of all.

'What was I supposed to do? Write to you and

say—by the way, guess what happened? Ruin your life too?'

He needed to reach her. 'My life was ruined when you wrote to me and told me never to come back.'

She shook her head. Not wanting to hear that. 'I was scared. Scared what my father would do to you. He warned me he'd ruin you if I contacted you. Ruin your family, who still worked for him. And I was scared that, if I told you, you'd never do the things you wanted to do. I know how important moving up in life was for you, Rory. I didn't want your bitterness and disappointment to be my fault if you'd come back to look after me.' She looked away. 'Then it was too late. I didn't want to talk about it. I still don't.'

'You were more important than my career.' It was his turn to deny. But, in all honesty, would he have had that clarity in his youth? 'I would never have blamed you. We would have made it somehow.' He reached out his hand to her. 'Kate, I would have been there for you. I'm here now.'

She ignored it. 'It's too late for us, Rory. I don't want a husband. When my father dies I'll sell Jabiru Station and go back to Perth. It's time to go back. I'll open a refuge for pregnant women, plaster its availability everywhere, give young women options that they might not otherwise get.'

It couldn't end this way. 'You can do that and still see me.'

She shook her head at him like he was a child. Like the child he was beginning to feel against her implacable wisdom. 'You're still in love with someone who doesn't exist, Rory. The sixteen-year-old girl you left. I'm not that girl. I never will be again.'

This couldn't be it. After the glimmer of hope when he'd found out she'd never married. After the rapport they'd shared in flashes only today. There could be more of those. 'I could love the woman she's become.'

One decisive shake of her head. 'I don't think so.' Then she lifted her chin and said the saddest thing yet. 'Because if I can't love myself how can you?'

Oh, Kate. What had he done? 'You were too young to cope with that on your own. I was careless and unprepared for what happened that afternoon but I should have come back to check you were all right. I'm sorry I let you down, Kate.'

'I don't want to talk about it any more, Rory. Just know…' here she paused, and Rory knew he wasn't going to like what was coming '…I've been powerless. I've been excluded in consultation on what affects me and, worst of all, unable to keep myself or my child safe, and I won't ever be like that again. I am in charge of my own destiny.' She turned her face to look into the fire. 'I'm going to run my own life and nothing or no one is going to change that.'

That finality struck into his heart like a shard of ice.

But it pricked his anger as well. That wasn't fair. Rory frowned. 'I'm not trying to change you, Kate, but I'm not a nobody, harassing you. I'm your friend, the man who wanted to marry you, someone who knows you inside and out— or did—ten years ago. I loved you, Kate, as you were, and I could love you as you are now. I'm just trying to be here for you.'

He took her hand and, when she didn't respond, he slipped his arm around her and drew her close. 'I'm not going to pressure you. Ever. Though maybe we could call a truce. Share some grief that affects both of us.'

After the initial stiffness she did slightly relax against him as she thought about it. It did affect both of them. It was a new concept that maybe she'd been too buried in her own misery to think about before.

She hadn't given in, but truce was a good word and sharing the memories of that time with Rory, the only person she had ever shared them with, was painful but strangely healing. She thought for the first time of Rory as her baby's other parent. And for her possibly selfish assumption that it wouldn't matter to him if he didn't know. Maybe she did owe him an apology.

'Kate—' he squeezed her hand '—is it too late to give our son a name? It's so sad we can't call him anything. Acknowledge our baby as a real person who will always be a part of our lives, no matter how fleeting.'

The sting of tears Rory's comment caused made Kate blink and she wished just once she could turn towards him and sob in his arms. Why couldn't she cry?

A name? For their son who flew away ten

years ago. She looked at Rory, in his eyes such concern that she realised he worried his question hurt her. The ice inside melted a little more. 'I always liked Cameron,' she said softly, and squeezed his hand back.

'Cameron Onslow-McIver.' He lifted her fingers to his mouth and turned her hand to kiss her palm. The gentlest benediction. 'Our son.'

So they sat there as the fire died, occasionally talking but mostly just leaning into each other and Kate could feel the easing of the burden she'd carried for so many lonely years. That pain would never go but Rory had not done the one thing she'd feared above everything. He hadn't said her baby didn't matter.

CHAPTER SEVEN

IT WAS six a.m. and the sun was dusting the horizon pink when Rory woke. He doubted Kate had slept well because the stretcher bed had creaked all night and he'd bet she wished she'd swapped places with him in his quiet swag.

He rolled over onto his back and stared at the tree branches lacing the sky at the edge of his vision. He needed to find a way to keep open the chink in Kate's barriers against him. Maybe then he could also ease the burden that Kate had carried for so long.

He could almost deal with the fact she didn't want to spend the rest of her life with him. Almost.

What he couldn't deal with was the memory of that despair in Kate's face and the realisation that she'd done it alone when he should have been there. No wonder she hadn't wanted to see him again.

He'd made decisions that had affected her without thinking of her choices. No matter that leaving to make his fortune for her had been in her best interests.

He sighed. Had it really been, though? Rory wondered sardonically to himself, not for the first time since he'd returned to the Kimberley. Hadn't it all been about him feeling inferior to Kate's family and needing to prove he could be bigger and better than they were? Were those goals—top man in the state, paramedic extraordinaire, independently wealthy to equal the Onslows—really for Kate or his own gratification?

It wasn't a very nice picture he'd just painted

and he doubted an apology would cut for what Kate had been through.

No wonder she hadn't wanted to tell him about what had happened. He had to break down that reserve and it had better be before they got back to Jabiru or he'd never reach her. Because one thing was clear after last night—he still wanted Kate—and he wanted all of her.

Rory rose and rolled his swag. Kate was up before he'd poked the fire back into life for a mug of tea. 'Sleep well?'

'Hmm, no,' she mumbled as she walked past him into the scrub. He smiled to himself. So his Kate still wasn't a morning person.

They sipped tea and ate fruit before he tackled the truck. They jacked it up and Kate rolled the spare across to him, passing tools and clearing up when she wasn't needed. Not a bad team, Rory thought, and they smiled with less tension between them as they went about their tasks. The truck was rolling within the hour.

Kate glanced at her watch. 'You still think we'll get home today?'

'We'll give it our best shot and as long as it hasn't rained somewhere we don't know about.'

'This truck can manage most terrain.' Kate patted the dash.

'That's my girl.' Rory smiled at her and she frowned a warning at him.

'Figure of speech,' he said and Kate just shook her head. But he suspected there may have been a tiny smile there. It was a start. They used to laugh a lot together.

One thing he didn't understand. 'So if you hate your father so much, how can you stand to come back now?'

She huffed a sigh. 'Why do we have to talk about me all the time? Let's talk about you.'

He did understand her reluctance but this was

important. 'I'd really like to know, Kate. I'll probably fly out of here as soon as the weather settles. Never bother you again, if that's what you want.' Lord, he hoped not. 'But you can't change that I do care about you. Or that I have some right to know why you cut me out of your life.'

She wouldn't meet his eyes. 'You do?'

'You knew the letter you sent me was a lie and yet you let your father back in.'

She flicked a stray hair out of her face. 'Don't start again. I don't need your opinion on what I do.'

'I think you do.' He glanced at her. 'Besides, with that mean and nasty attitude you have, there can't be too many people who love you.'

She smothered a laugh and Rory smiled with her. He'd been the only one who'd dared to poke fun at her and he'd bet that hadn't changed much.

She screwed her face up at him and grudgingly considered his question. 'Why did I come back?' She shrugged. 'Because he's my father and he asked me to come home. And he's dying. And maybe I need to lay some of my own ghosts—' she looked at him '—like you did.'

That was a start. 'Fair enough.' He met her eyes and then looked back at the road. 'So why are you working at Jabiru Township?'

She shrugged again and he could tell she wanted this conversation finished. 'There's a need there. The clinic is my statement that I do my own thing. My father doesn't control me but I'll still see him.' She glared at the windscreen as if her father were on the other side.

She went on, 'As we're dissecting my emotions, I think that being there for Lucy yesterday could help a lot with closure, especially as there's a good outcome.'

Thank you, God, for brief windows of enlightenment, Rory thought, but he had so much more to fathom. He wanted to ask questions but she'd slipped into a reverie. He didn't want to disturb the flow of her thoughts as he tried to grasp what was important to this new Kate.

As he'd hoped, she went on. 'Lucy made the same mistakes as me but she was more fortunate. Does that make me a bad mother because my baby died and Lucy's didn't?' She turned to Rory and he saw the moment she allowed herself to consider some absolution. She shook her head with relief. 'Thank goodness Lucy's baby is okay.'

Rory continued the concept she only seemed to be grasping now. 'We both know that young mums and toxaemia happen pretty fast, sometimes with devastating results, but you couldn't have known that when you were sixteen. Of course you were unlucky.'

Rory went on, 'You made a good call for Lucy, Kate. Leaving Jabiru, not waiting until the weather set in; it would have been easy to hold off a decision until too late.'

Kate chewed her lip as she remembered. 'I was so scared for Lucy and her baby.'

'Well, you didn't show it. Despite your own doubts. I thought you were amazing during the birth.'

She squeezed her eyes shut for a moment, as if to block out the memory. 'I lost it for a second.' She shook her head and shuddered. 'It all flashed back at me, you know, I've never had that before and, although everything was okay in the end, I never want to have those feelings again.'

'Maybe you needed that moment to move on. I think you're still too hard on yourself.'

'Maybe. Maybe not.' She shook her head. 'I know birth is run by nature. Without interference, it's designed to run smoothly and that's what happened to Lucy. Lucky Lucy.'

'Lucky Lucy to have you.'

She frowned as if the thought remained un-palatable and brushed his comment away. 'Flattery. You're wasting your time because compliments mean nothing. And you're still not invading my life.'

'Damn.' He felt like a spy peering over the top of the wall into a forbidden city and he couldn't help but smile at her back-pedalling. 'I thought I was doing well there.'

Too well, Kate thought, *that's the problem,* and she turned to look out of the window. She needed to keep some barriers up and Rory was systematically lowering them one by one. She wasn't throwing away ten years of stoicism and independence because of a few kind words but it was hard not to slip back into that old security of his presence.

Rory slowed the truck and she looked ahead as they approached the first of the river cross-ings. This had been the deeper one on the way with Lucy and the river height had gained another six inches. As a cemented causeway it wasn't as treacherous as a riverbank crossing but still the flow was much faster than before.

He pulled up and turned the engine off and they both climbed out to look. At least the rain had stopped and the weather was heading towards a mild day shrouded in cloud.

The roar of the water at the rapids further down almost drowned out the flow in front of them across the causeway. Rory knelt to pull off his riding boots and roll his trousers while Kate chewed her lip.

Past the causeway in the deeper part of the river the water looked to have a strong current in the middle and wild eddies down the side that swooped under overhanging trees.

Any other time it would be pleasant under those trees when not in flood but at the moment the branches swept the water and tangled anything that floated. With the amount of water that gushed past, it would relentlessly bombard anything, or anybody, washed into the branches with tons of never-ending water.

'You sure you want to wade across there?'

Rory looked up at her from under his brows. 'You just watch for crocs, though this crossing's not as bad as the Pentecost for salties.'

'The water looks fast.' My word, it did, thought Kate, as she scanned the riverbank for movement and then followed a piece of bark that scooted past her and twirled around as if unseen hands under the water were spinning it in a game.

'If I can't walk the causeway, I won't drive it,' he said, 'but I want to get closer to home than this. Don't you?'

Kate agreed but it was more difficult than she'd expected to watch Rory prepare to take that risk.

They both looked downstream where the river

widened and shallowed and the trees poked out of the riverbed near the rushing middle.

Rory smiled reassuringly but Kate wasn't feeling reassured and something he must have seen in her face made his eyes narrow. 'I'm not planning to, but if I do get swept away I'll be able to get out down there.' He pointed. 'I'll be fine.' He held her gaze. 'Do not come to save me if I slide down.'

Kate had seen the clearer area he'd indicated but it still flowed too fast for comfort. The real rapids came after that and the thunder from them was what they could hear. Then, if he didn't manage to stop himself, there was a fifty foot waterfall that plunged into the gorge to look forward to.

The images were far too graphic for Kate. 'Let's not play that game.'

There was an edge to his voice. 'Promise you'll stay out of the water, Kate.'

In all the years she'd known him, the only time she'd ever seen Rory really angry had been when she'd put herself in danger. The way he said it reminded her of a time she'd always blushed to remember.

That night Rory told her not to follow him out to the shed to save the duck she'd befriended from the chopping block.

Rory was so nearly caught by Kate's father, except Kate slipped into the shed and turned out the lights and he was able to get away. Her father never was sure if a dingo had got the duck or Kate had been responsible but Rory was livid she'd put herself at risk. He flayed her with his anger so fiercely that she almost wished he'd shaken her instead; he didn't speak to her for days. But she would have done it again if she'd needed to.

* * *

Today was like that. She couldn't guarantee it.

'Well, don't get washed away.'

Rory grinned at her. 'Kate. You really do care.'

Grrr. Typical man, laughing at danger. If men took fewer risks there'd be less danger. They were so stupid sometimes. 'Oh, I care, but then I'd care if you were an animal.' She pretended to ponder it. 'Probably more.'

Rory looked suitably dashed. 'Gee, thanks.'

He gave up his attempt to roll his jeans high enough and moved back to the truck, where he shucked them down and threw them on the driver's seat.

'Now do you care?' He posed, hands on the strongly muscled thighs of his tanned legs, elbows bent like a male model as Kate tried not to see the whipcord body beneath his black boxers and shirt tails. Rory had certainly grown up.

She shrugged and looked away to hide her

eyes. 'Maybe. I'd probably care as much as an animal. Now, stop stressing me and move it,' Kate said and turned her back. Actually, it was for her own protection because Rory looked far too sexy and dangerous, and too dear to lose. Yet, despite their predicament, she was beginning to wish he'd taken off his shirt as well as his jeans so she could see what she couldn't help imagining. What she should be thinking instead was how she could save him if he needed help.

'Enough joking,' he said and Kate felt her heart rate pick up with a thump in her chest as Rory turned to enter the water. Her palms truly began to sweat.

'Be careful, Rory.' She had a bad feeling about this.

He approached the edge. 'Yes, ma'am.' He looked back at her once more as he entered the water. 'Do watch for mysterious logs with eyes.'

'Absolutely.' Kate was deadly serious—they both were—and she scanned the banks again before she watched him wade in.

Rory edged across, one step at a time. The water attempted to sweep him sideways but he leaned into it, strong thighs braced against the torrent. Once he stumbled slightly when his foot slipped into a crumbled section and Kate stifled a scream but he recovered well. He threw her a one-eyebrow-raised glance and continued on.

Kate rested her hand over the pulse in her throat—she could feel the beat against her fingers—and took shallow sips of air until Rory finally emerged on the other side.

The causeway was deep but the truck would handle it. Rory started back and Kate watched his every step, which was why she didn't see the branch until it was too late.

'Watch the log, Rory,' she yelled and he twisted

to see, maybe even thinking it was a crocodile, and lost his footing and the branch collided with his legs as he tried to regain his balance.

Rory was skittled into the water like a tenpin by a ball and Kate screamed his name as his head bobbed under the water and then resurfaced.

The speed of the water carried him swiftly down the swirling river and Kate scrambled along the side of the bank as she desperately tried to keep up with him through the scrub.

Her heart pounded in her ears and she couldn't see where he'd gone until she climbed out onto a fallen tree that overhung the river. The trunk stretched a third of the way across the torrent but where it dipped into the water she couldn't keep her balance and she had to sit down to edge along the trunk so she could peer out over the river.

Rory was hooked on a tree root that curled around him like an arthritic hand out of the bed of the river. It tangled his shirt as the water flowed over his face and head and he disappeared under the water. Then he reappeared, shook his head to clear it and glanced up to where Kate was overhanging the torrent.

He saw what she was about to do almost before she knew herself and she only just heard his distant, 'No, Kate!' as she launched herself into the dark water and struck out across the current towards Rory's wooden island.

The cold water took her breath as she fought to stay upright and the occasional rounded boulder in the bed thudded into her knees and buttocks as she bounced down the river. She'd be a mass of bruises tomorrow if they lived to tell the tale.

The current's strength gave her little say about direction and she tried to grasp the rocks she passed to steer towards Rory and only succeeded in breaking off her nails. When she looked towards him he'd lost his shirt, was free of entrapment and had managed to stand against the torrent with his back against the mid-section of the root.

She had about three seconds to get closer to him or she was going to shoot past and end up down the rapids and over the waterfall herself. A quiet space in her brain was tutting and saying that she should have listened to Rory and waited for him to get himself out.

She didn't know where Rory's arm came from but his hand fastened onto her shoulder like a vice and he heaved her across to him and into his arms as if she were a floating twig until they were both flattened face to face against the root with the force of the water.

He hugged her so tightly against him she almost couldn't breathe. 'If we don't die here I am going to kill you,' he ground out, and his mouth crushed down on hers with no gentleness at all, a plunging ravishment that tumbled her into more of a maelstrom than the water around her. Then he turned her in his arms and pulled her back against him again as her head swam.

Her teeth chattered with the shock of her near miss and the feel of Rory's warm, solid strength behind her made her realise how close she'd been to shooting past. But most of all there was the imprint of Rory's mouth—hot and dangerous—and the livid emotion she'd seen in his eyes that warned he wasn't done yet.

'Move where I move,' he snapped out and, still stunned by the bruising kiss, she nodded and did what she was told for the first time in a lot of years.

Rory braced like a standing stone behind her, solid and immovable to lean on, as she pulled each thigh sideways against the swirling strength of the water, step by exhausting step, until the water became shallower and she could just stand on her own. The fear of being washed away had been gradually replaced each step closer to the bank by the awareness that Rory was a thundercloud behind her and he hadn't loosened his iron grip on her shoulder.

He turned her, none too gently, to face him again and she could see his lips compressed together as he struggled for control.

'Just once!' He shook her and she could feel the barely leashed fury that struggled to be free. 'Do what you're told!'

She looked away from this hard-faced man she barely knew and yes, she'd got it wrong, she should have listened. She tried bravado and glared back at him. 'I had to do what my instinct told me to.'

Not a good choice. Rory looked more incensed than before. 'Instinct? Instinct?' He shook her again. 'You could have died. Your instinct is to do whatever I say is a bad idea.'

'I'm sorry I didn't listen to you, Rory.' She looked into his face, searching for some glimmer of the Rory who would hug her to him and say it was all right.

Rory stared down at her. 'You could have died.' He shook his head and she saw what she had done to him and she couldn't stop the sting of tears that gathered but didn't fall.

'I'm sorry,' she whispered and she leaned up and kissed his cold, hard lips that would not respond. She tried again, pushing her mouth against his, moulding the chiselled edges of his mouth with her own and still he remained immovable. She lifted her arms and pulled the back of his head towards hers, ran her hands down his cheeks to their joined mouths, as if drawing all the emotion to their lips, until eventually he shuddered and gathered her fiercely into his arms and kissed her back, not quite as fiercely as he had out in the water but powerfully, and in a way that left her in no doubt that he would like to do more than just kiss her—and not in the way the Rory of ten years ago had kissed her. This man knew what response he wanted and how to draw it from her. Kate felt as if she'd been swept into a raging torrent again, only this time she didn't want to be rescued. She wanted to drown!

When he finally lifted his mouth away she could barely stand.

He gave her another hug and she closed her eyes as she wrapped her arms around his solid strength and hugged him back to regain strength in her limbs. 'Let's not do that again.'

'The river or the kiss?' His voice still held many undercurrents but he put her away from him with some semblance of control. 'Come on. Before the river comes up any higher.' Rory's fingers cradled the small of her back in a protective gesture that was almost an apology for the harshness of the kiss and she realised he was panting a little.

The fact that Rory had acted so out of character showed her, as little else could have, just how much he cared. Still. The implications of that were too huge but for the moment she'd just be glad they were both safe.

They pushed through the scrub at the side of the river until they made it back to the truck, where she handed him a towel and took one herself as she turned her back, for her own protection, while he shucked off his boxers. He must have dried off and pulled his jeans on quickly because he was back in the truck when Kate turned around.

'Let's get this crossing over with,' he said, 'and then you can change.'

As soon as Kate was in the truck Rory let out the clutch and they crawled down into the causeway and chugged with remarkable ease through the water. A bow wave surged in front of the bonnet, Kate lifted her feet above the wash that came through the doors to ankle height, then they both opened their doors to let the water out as the wheels of the truck climbed up the other side.

Rory whistled. 'Very close. Wouldn't want to be much deeper than that.' He pulled over and she slid out and exchanged her wet clothes for a dry shirt and shorts she had in her overnight pack.

When she climbed back in she was glad he didn't mention their recent session in the river. She didn't think she could talk about it just yet without shivering. Probably shock. She fought to keep her voice steady. 'Doesn't look good for the Pentecost.'

Kate began to realise they would have to camp again tonight if the river was flooded. And what would happen between them after the high emotions of the past half an hour she had no idea and not a little trepidation.

They were talking, fairly naturally now, considering, and neither mentioned their close escape or the events afterwards and she hoped her concern and relief for Rory's safety hadn't made him think she was easy prey. Because she wasn't, or wouldn't be by the time they stopped this evening, would she?

CHAPTER EIGHT

IT HAD to be ten minutes since they'd last spoken and Kate's imagination made her squirm. Surely Rory might be reliving her stupidity in his mind again. The more she thought about it, the more she cringed. What had she expected to achieve by jumping in?

The sensible thing would have been to stay on dry land like she'd been told—that sanctimonious voice in her head had to repeat—she could have thrown him a rope or even got help if he'd been too hurt to move and not set herself up for a last trip down the river.

Suddenly she couldn't stand her own one-sided dialogue of his disapproval or the silence in the truck any longer. 'I'm sorry, Rory.'

He seemed intent on the road ahead and when he didn't reply she cringed even more and changed the subject. She went on quietly, 'How long now until the Pentecost?'

'Still about two hours. The rain's coming down again so it depends on the creeks we have to cross.' There was no hint of censure in Rory's voice when he answered so he must have been concentrating on the road which, she had to admit, was pretty churned up. Not the only thing churned up, she thought ruefully. She really needed to get a grip.

He went on, 'After that little adventure I'm not driving across waterways in the dark.'

She'd drink to that. 'So do you think we'll have to camp again?'

He looked at her and smiled, and suddenly her world was back the right way. She didn't want to think about how much she'd come to depend on Rory's unfailing good humour.

'Not necessarily,' he said. 'If you want to do something radical we could take another ten mile detour to Xanadu and stay the night at the high-end resort up there.'

She'd agree to almost anything if it meant he'd forgiven her—but Xanadu? She'd read about that. 'It costs the price of a small car to stay there for one night.'

'True. But we haven't stayed anywhere together, so if you divide it by ten years it isn't much to spend for a couple.' He had a smile in his eyes because he knew she'd bite.

That was taking it too far. 'We're not a couple.'

'So we camp or split it.'

Rory grinned to himself. She hadn't expected him to offer to split it. Not that he needed her money. He'd made some very shrewd invest-ment decisions before Perth had taken off as a real estate boom town, but it amused him that he had her off balance, which was a big turn-around from the back foot he'd been on since before their adventure.

They needed a little light relief after the recent events. He still shuddered to remember the sight of Kate launching herself into the river to save him. He couldn't remember when he had ever been more frightened—or more angry.

Imagine if he hadn't been able to reach her as she'd gone past. The idea brought the nausea to his throat again and he dragged his thoughts away from that scenario. For himself to fall in it had been a bloody nuisance, but the degree of danger Kate had been in made his blood run cold.

It seemed she'd forgiven him for the angry kiss he'd punished her with but it had been that or he'd have paddled her behind as soon as he hit dry land—something he would never believe he'd want to do to Kate.

And she knew it. He'd actually like some time to think about the expression on her face as she'd looked when they'd both finally got out of the river. Stuff of dreams. And that fierce hug. He could still feel her arms around him and it felt damn good.

She nodded slowly. 'If you can afford it. Or we could do the tent cabins, which are cheaper.'

He was glad to think of other things. It was sweet of her to be concerned for the cost and he was tempted to tell her she needn't worry but he kept his mouth shut.

He frowned. Obviously he still had some inferiority issues he needed to work through. He was finding out a lot about himself today.

Kate went on, 'Hang the expense. I never spend anything and haven't spoilt myself for years.' She frowned. 'What if they're booked out?'

He patted the phone on the dash. 'We could find out.'

Kate glanced out at the deepening gloom as the day edged towards another night. 'Hot showers. Hot food.' She glanced at him with a smug expression. 'Separate rooms.'

Separate rooms? Rory thought. Now, that's a shame. There'd be less chance of her throwing herself into his arms and he couldn't deny he'd desperately love to sit with Kate in his arms, even if only to soak in the fact that she was fine. It had been a long eventful day with some potential for more than emotional fallout.

Kate smiled at him. 'Let's do it. Sounds too good to miss.'

'Good.' He looked across and then back at the road. 'I was thinking if we stayed until after lunch tomorrow we could do a spot of bush walking. Check out the gorges and waterfalls because after the rain they'll be spectacular. That'd give the Pentecost more time to go down and we'd still be back to Jabiru before dark.'

She chewed her lip and he wanted to put his hand out and stop her. Not those beautiful lips—lips that he wanted to do better things with now that he'd had a recent taste. Finally she stopped biting. 'Maybe we could have a few hours before we leave tomorrow morning.'

Kate rifled through the glovebox and came up with directions and phone numbers of all the stations and refuelling stops along the road. She found Xanadu. 'Here's the number.'

She dialled and, after a few quick sentences, it was done. 'Should take us about an hour to get there.

He thought she was finding it easier to talk to him. At least she'd stopped twisting her hands. Maybe the emotions of the last few hours had put things in a different perspective for her too. He hoped so.

'Time to kill while we get there,' she said.

'Want to enlarge on the ten years between then and now, on your side for a change, Rory?'

Did he? Not really. What had he done? Not much else except work. His job had been a strange one but had suited him by blocking out his loss of Kate.

'It's been absorbing,' he said. 'The best parts are the good friends. You need them to face the tragedies, so they're a saving grace. But even mates can't stop the human emotion from taking its toll.' Nothing would.

'Though lately that camaraderie's been lost with my move to administration and away from road work. The price of rapid advancement up the ranks, I guess, so I miss that.'

He sighed, and pondered, to nut it out as much for himself as for her. 'Work was work. There pretty well every day and most nights.'

She raised her eyebrows. 'It sounds like you were on a mission.'

He looked at her. She still didn't get it. 'Funny, that.'

'You must have had some fun.' She frowned and he wondered if the frown was because he'd had little fun or because of the little he'd had. It amused him that she could be even slightly jealous.

He raised his eyebrows. 'Brief snatches.'

'Like Sybil?'

He'd been right. He nodded and squashed the urge to laugh. 'I did wonder if we'd get back to Sybil.'

She gazed out of the window nonchalantly; her turned shoulder said she didn't care if he answered. He held off until she couldn't resist. 'So?' she said.

Serious now, he stopped teasing her. 'Like a lot of other professions, there's mental wear and tear, those moments of despair at the useless loss of life.' Lost faces that tore at him at night, alone in his bed, until he'd gone out searching for anything to blot out the pictures he couldn't rid. On top of the loss of the love of his life.

'For a while, Sybil helped.' Come upon in a moment of weakness, and so difficult to extricate himself from.

Best not talk about Sybil. 'But there were delightful patients who popped up in the most unexpected places who made everything we did seem worthwhile.' He turned to look at her. Deliberately blotting those they'd lost with different images.

'I like the mix of people I come into contact with as a health worker. Young kids are hard work but satisfying because they're so frightened and we can help that, then there's old men with dry-as-a-stick humour who downplay their illnesses so you have to watch them pretty closely. Sweet old ladies are so apologetic for calling when in fact they should have called hours ago. Then a week later they'll drop into the ambulance station to say thank you with home-made scones and real jam.'

He could see she was absorbed in his stories while he considered it all pretty normal. He smiled and shook his head. 'I love old ladies.'

She laughed. 'I think there's a name for that.' She raised her eyebrows suggestively.

'Be nice.' He pretended to glare at her and she giggled. Something he'd thought he'd never hear his Kate do again.

'And the occasional birth,' she prompted.

'Trust a midwife to ask that.' He thought of Lucy's birth. 'Babies too.'

Kate tilted her head. 'So what was all this in aid of, Rory? Where did you see yourself going when you finally made it? Did you sock away all your money to fund some elusive dream?'

'Maybe.' The thought struck him. Good grief.

Had he? Suddenly everything was clear. That was what he'd been planning and he hadn't even known it. Jabiru Station?

His head was spinning; he needed time to think that all through again. Like about a week. Certainly not now.

He steered the conversation away to safer topics. 'Enough about me. Tell me about your midwifery. You said you went to uni. Where did you work when you finished?'

She frowned at the switch of topic but answered him. 'Still Perth.'

He shook his head at the idea of both of them never passing at some hospital or other. 'I was there, too.'

'And Sybil.' Kate looked out of the window again.

They didn't need complications that didn't exist. 'Sybil again?'

She laughed. 'Just teasing.'

'I'm happy to share if you're interested.' He didn't want lies between them. 'Sybil was in my life for a brief while. She's a hothouse flower, our Sybil. Likes to sway along, bask in the sun, have new petals supplied by men who fancy her. It didn't last long, but there was a while there where she saved my sanity.'

'Then I forgive her.'

It was a joking comment, but something in the tone of Kate's voice had nothing to do with Sybil. It had to do with knowing what feeling really down was about. About using anything and anyone to get out of that hole and see the light again. Surviving.

It was coming home to him just how much Kate had survived. His voice dropped. 'I guess we're both survivors.'

'Hope those people up there are too!' Kate had looked ahead and seen the rolled vehicle before Rory. He bit back a frustrated sigh and focused on what the scenario could be. Would this trip never end? He braked and stopped as they came upon the wreckage. It didn't look too bad but you never knew.

In fact, maybe it had been time to shut down the conversation they were in. He opened his door and sprinted through the rain to peer into the front window of the Jeep as it lay on its side.

'You okay in here?'

'Yeah.' The young man poked his head out of the window like a jack-in-the-box. 'I'm waiting for the rain to clear before I try winching it back onto its wheels.'

Rory peered through into the vehicle. 'Anyone in the back?'

'Nah. Just me. Embarrassed. Swerved for a bullock and flipped it in the mud.'

Rory nodded. 'Want a hand?'

'I'd appreciate it.' The driver climbed out awkwardly and Kate could see he was younger than her but laconic in his predicament. Rory tilted his head and watched the way the young man held his arm tight against his chest.

'I'm Rory. This is Kate.'

'Leslie.' He held out his good arm and Rory shook it. He nodded at Kate.

Rory pointed at his injury. 'Hurt your arm, have you, Leslie? Do you mind if I have a look?'

Leslie winced as he lifted it. 'Banged it on the wheel when we went over.'

Rory ran his fingers lightly over the swelling in the forearm. 'I'd say you're lucky you didn't have it out the window, mate.'

Leslie waggled his fingers without too much effort but couldn't move his forearm from in front of his chest.

Rory raised his eyebrows at Kate and she nodded and opened the back of the ambulance. When she returned with a triangular bandage Rory carefully lifted Leslie's arm and between them they supported the arm in a makeshift sling.

'I'd say you've broken one of those bones in your forearm.'

'Thought so.' Leslie shrugged and then winced as his shoulder moved. 'It's my right arm so I can still change gears. I'll survive.'

'Where're you heading?'

'I'm a ringer at Xanadu. Camp's about three miles this side of the resort.'

They could help. 'When we get your Jeep on its feet we'll give you a lift, if you like. We're heading that way. Kate can drive the ambulance and we'll follow in yours.'

'Don't want to be any trouble.'

Kate laughed. 'We can see that. Just humour us, okay. So, tell me, you allergic to anything, Leslie?'

'Not that I know of.'

She smiled. 'Then here's two painkillers. Tell

me if your injured hand goes colder than the other one.' She gave him the pills, which he put in his mouth, and then she handed him a bottle of water to sip. She turned to the Jeep. 'What do you want me to do, Rory?'

'I'll connect the winch and watch the pull if you take the ambulance back slowly in low range.'

'Done.'

A few minutes later, Leslie's old vehicle was back on its wheels, Rory had Leslie tucked in beside him and Kate followed behind until they turned off on the Xanadu Road.

Fifteen minutes later they handed Leslie over to the foreman at the camp and Kate drove the rest of the way in the last of the fading light.

As they passed through the resort gateway Rory stretched his arms over his head as much as the roof allowed. 'This has been a very busy two days,' he groaned and Kate smiled.

'True. But the company's been great.'

Was that a positive comment? 'Shucks. You're just saying that.'

She actually grinned at him. 'Yep. I'm hoping you'll buy me dinner.'

He tossed his head. 'Who's the heiress?'

She shrugged. 'So what do you make, Mr Hotshot?'

He raised his eyebrows suggestively. 'Enough for dinner.'

She nodded, as if something had been confirmed. 'Then you're on. But we share the cost of the rooms.' Kate sighed at the thought. 'Right after a hot bath.'

They pulled up under the portico and the concierge greeted them like royalty and indicated that their ambulance would be cared for like the Rolls-Royce it wasn't.

Kate smothered a laugh as she pulled the duffel bag of spare clothes out of the back of the truck. The bag was whisked from her arms to be carried by another assistant and she could do nothing but join Rory as they walked up the stairs, where they were met by the manager.

Within what seemed like seconds they were registered and personally escorted to their suites.

Kate hung back a little and whispered to Rory, 'I think we should have stayed in the tent section. I'm feeling a little underdressed.'

'I bet they can cater for that.' He smiled across at her. 'But you look gorgeous to me.'

'Don't go there, Rory. And I mean it. This is too elegant for an overnight stay.'

He held up his hands. 'Fine. But just relax. Soak in your bath and we'll meet in an hour. We can eat on a private veranda if you want.'

Which was all very well, Kate thought an hour later, admittedly more relaxed and glowing pink from the hot water, but her khaki trousers and white shirt just didn't do it for her.

When she heard the knock on the door, she glanced once more at the mirror and shrugged. It was only one night.

It wasn't Rory at the door. A young girl stood there, beautifully made-up and wearing the resort staff cheongsam. She held a fuchsia-pink silk sheath in her arms. 'From Mr McIver, Miss Onslow.'

Kate opened her mouth to say wrong room when she heard her name. She'd kill him. What was she supposed to do? Good manners won. 'Thank you,' she said. Serve him right if it cost him a month's salary. She took the dress from the girl and shut the door.

It was beautiful. She rested the material against her cheek and slid it back and forth like a whisper. She'd never been one for fancy clothes and still refused any money from her father.

She looked in the mirror. She could wear

her pride or this. She looked again. That was ridiculous.

The dress won.

When Kate opened her door Rory forgot to breathe. Dark swathes of velvet hair were loose around her shoulders, the first time he'd seen her hair out in ten years, and he hoped not the last. Her mouth pouted sexily in fuchsia like the dress, and then the dress…

No bra. He sucked the breath in because light-headedness was no way to handle the next couple of hours—but my Lord. Rory gulped.

'Come in, Rory,' she said and directed him in with her hand, her mind obviously elsewhere as she searched for her key.

'I like your dress.' He looked around the room, out of the door to the magnificent view of the gorge below, at the huge king-sized bed and quickly away, anywhere except at the fuchsia silk outline of her alert nipples.

'The room's lovely, isn't it?'

'Very.' Monosyllables might be all he could manage at the moment.

'Oh, here it is!' She held the key up triumphantly. Then she looked at him and he still must have been staring. 'Thank you for the dress. I hope you've left enough in your wallet for dinner.' Obviously she'd come to peace with his presumption in buying it.

'Luckily dinner's included in the room rate. Table d'hôte gourmet and open bar. Served where you want. Any preferences?'

She blinked. 'Wow. They didn't have anything like this around when we grew up here.'

'That's the high-end market for you.'

'You seem to know a lot about it.'

'If I'd ever been here I would have looked you up and maybe discovered you were in Perth.'

The heat from the gaze he ran over her was enough to have Kate wishing she hadn't been so silly as to put on the dress or send for the matching lippy. And leave off her sensible bra.

She looked him up and down. He had a white jacket over a black shirt and black trousers, very debonair for a boy from the Outback. She'd bet that hadn't been in the duffel bag either. Maybe he was more financially secure than she'd thought.

She cleared her throat. 'We could eat in the open air part of the restaurant.' Might be safer, she thought, and she had the feeling he could read her mind. Somehow the balance had shifted again.

'Fine,' he said. 'I understand the view is magnificent.' She'd swear he was laughing at her.

Kate's enormous room was suddenly stifling despite the breeze wafting the curtains. 'Let's go, then.'

They chose to sit on the veranda outside the restaurant with its glass roof showcasing the stars that looked down on them. Rory pulled her chair out, much to the chagrin of the maître d', but at least he smiled at the man. 'I'm sorry. I wanted to do that.'

Kate dipped her head to examine the menu and hide the blush from Rory's comment. This was getting out of hand but a tiny part of her found the danger intoxicating.

'Champagne?' Rory raised those wicked eyebrows of his and Kate shook her head.

I'm heady enough, she thought. 'I'd prefer to keep my wits about me.'

'Perhaps sparkling apple juice?' the waiter suggested, and Kate nodded.

'The same.' Rory wasn't to be outdone. 'Though we may decide on a wine later with dessert.'

The waiter left as they dawdled over the

menus. Kate looked around and shook her head. 'This place is incredible.'

'I'm glad we came. It's totally different from where we would have slept.'

'It's different from where you were going to sleep. I was going to have the comfortable stretcher in the back again.'

'Weren't we going to toss for it?'

She shook her head. 'Heads or tails, it was mine.'

He smiled. 'You've become quite assertive, Miss Kate.'

'Survival.'

He lifted his glass and the ping of fine crystal made them both smile. Then his smile fell away. 'To survivors,' Rory said soberly.

By the time they'd finished the meal and enjoyed one glass of the smoothest port Rory had ever tasted, he was thinking of sitting on his hands to keep them under control.

Kate had relaxed enough to laugh and, when she did, his heart felt as if it was going to shatter into a million pieces like the stars through the glass above his head.

No wonder he hadn't settled in his life when that much feeling was tied up in one woman. And he hadn't even realised.

'Let's walk,' he said abruptly and he had Kate out of her chair before the waiter made it halfway across the room.

With his hand resting in the small of her back and her hair brushing his shoulder, it was as if the floodgates had opened and all the years of striving for fulfilment meant nothing. This was what he wanted—Kate with him, side by side as they walked along the gravel-strewn paths along the clifftop. Her tiny hand in his, and how the hell that had happened he didn't know, but he savoured every squeeze of her fingers.

Lush tropical foliage bathed in moonlight—moonlight that cascaded into the gorge below like the waterfall they could hear in the distance, and Kate, giggling beside him as he recited a sweet old lady story from his repertoire.

What was she thinking? What was she feeling? Could she see how good they were together and how they must be able to work things out? This was all too good to throw away.

They stopped in unison and turned. He looked down at her, bathed in silver with her precious face turned up to his and her eyes dark pools of invitation.

She seemed to sway slightly towards him so he kissed her gently, just to taste the promise. Her lips parted and suddenly she was pressing herself against him and her tongue fluttered against his so he kissed her with all the need of his own for the last ten years without Kate.

Then he kissed her for the letter, the return of

his ring, and finally for the fact that he had her in his arms at this moment.

Kate had known Rory was going to kiss her tonight. She'd been aware since they'd first sat down in the restaurant hours ago. Aware that this place out of time was the only chance they had to celebrate the past before they went their separate ways in the future.

She lifted her arms and it felt amazing just to reach up and clasp her hands behind his strong neck. To feel his arms go around her back and gather her closer, with his muscular chest solid and broad against her softness. This night had to last her a long time.

She looked up and he stared down, intent, sombre, questioning until his face moved closer; she couldn't help but sway towards him again and their lips rejoined as she closed her eyes.

Who needed vision when there was nothing she couldn't see with Rory's face there, his lips, his breath mingling with hers in that intricate dance that was solely theirs?

Homecoming yet not—the kiss had changed, they'd both grown up and this was no boy-girl kiss.

This was all man meets woman in paradise.

The kiss deepened, softened, deepened, and Kate began to lose the definition between the two. She strained closer and tightened her hold on his neck. He crushed her against him and she revelled in his long, strong hardness until Rory eased back.

For a brief moment in time there was almost a gap between them except for another quick sip and then he pulled away to grab her hand and, laughing, they ran six steps before they turned and kissed again. Moonlight madness consumed them both as they broke apart and ran another six before they stopped again. Kate could never remember feeling like this.

Behaving like this. By the time they were almost back at her room, they were heaving gasps of cool evening air laden with the scent of night flowers and the taste of lust.

Just a few steps more and they were in the hallway outside her door, where Kate crazily fumbled for her key in her door and then they were through, lips still fused, hands flying.

The first time was up against the wall, hiked dress, dropped trousers, insatiable and way too fast, though still time for Rory to protect her, yet, in some elemental way, not fast enough, and then it was over. Rory lifted her and carried her to the bed, where they lay together, wrapped in each other's arms.

They breathed in. Breathed out. Looked at each other and smiled. Then reached for each other again. Just to hold.

A little while later Rory led her to the huge shower with twin ceiling roses but they only needed one as the water streamed over her shoulders and he soaped her. This time was for slow discovery. Carefully loving her, totally rapt in his thorough task as he worshipped her and she put her face up to the water and let the years of drought wash away. Then she washed him, but after that he couldn't help but take her so they made love under the shower and then again back on the bed.

They slept entwined, or Kate slept. Rory stared at her dark head on his chest and stroked her shoulder. How had they wasted so much time? He still didn't know.

Had what they'd shared been too intense? Why did he feel the desperation in Kate that boded ill for their future when she'd just given him everything?

Did she finally understand they were meant to be together?

* * *

Kate woke with Rory sleeping beside her. So this was what she'd been missing all these years. No wonder she hadn't had the strength to fight without him all those years ago. She felt adored, protected, safe.

Then she pulled back as reality awoke. This was an interval in life, not a beginning.

That way lay weakness. Vulnerability. She only had to think of what they'd done last night to see how little control she had over herself when mixed with the headiness of being with Rory.

CHAPTER NINE

BREAKFAST was tropical splendour on the balcony. Kate was quiet compared to last night but he remembered she wasn't a morning person. Though she'd been showered and dressed when he'd woken. Which was a damn shame.

There was a lot about Kate he didn't know and some he did. But he wanted to know a whole more before they left this place. Like when could he make love with her again?

The rain had stopped through the night, there were gaps for the sun and it was hot, but the clouds were still heavy in the valleys and over the mountains.

They walked to Golden Gorge for a swim, only

a few hundred metres from the resort, and it was cool as they climbed down the leafy hundred steps to the deserted rock pool at the bottom.

The huge palm fronds and pandanus dipped over the turquoise waterhole and butterflies skimmed the water.

Rory looked around and then at his Kate, here in paradise. 'I'd forgotten how much I love the top country. There's nowhere like the gorges here.'

Kate nodded. 'I'm glad we stayed on today for a while. We might never get a chance to do this again.'

Rory shot a glance at her. 'I don't want to think that.'

She avoided his eyes. 'For this morning we won't.' She pulled off her T-shirt. 'Last in's a dirty dog.'

There was a mad flurry of discarded clothes and two simultaneous splashes as they hit the pool together but they surfaced apart. Kate shook the hair out of her eyes and swam with leisurely strokes towards the big rock at the edge, where she climbed out again, all long legs and curved arms and delicious sway of her hips and breasts. His mouth tightened for a moment as he saw the long bruise on her thigh from her rush down the river yesterday but he shook the ice away.

Rory wanted her then and there but he could see she had other thoughts so he trod water as he went back over her words with a feeling of sadness. She'd said they might never get this chance again!

It seemed last night hadn't changed anything except maybe helped a little towards Kate's healing process. He couldn't regret it if that was all this trip had accomplished—it had been worth it, though it had not been without cost to his own heart. But he guessed that was a small price to pay for what Kate had been through.

But the concept of leaving Kate was too huge to contemplate here.

Kate dived in again and swam under the waterfall that fell into the pool. She stood in it, letting the water pour over her shoulders like a freshwater mermaid and he allowed the future to float away as he soaked in the sight.

When she'd had enough she dived back towards him and grabbed his ankle as she swam under him. He allowed himself to be pulled along before she let go to surface and he swam after her.

She shook her head and the water splashed in his face. 'So, you wanna play tag, do you?'

Kate grinned at him. 'I was always a better swimmer than you.'

'Try me now!' He dared her with one eyebrow raised and she turned to swim away. He easily caught her. 'Try again?'

She wiped the water from her eyes. 'Of course.'

This time he gave her a bigger head start but then easily caught her again.

She frowned. 'Been working out, McIver?'

'Could have.' He swam closer. 'Come here.'

She eyed him warily. 'Why?'

'I always wanted to kiss underwater. I need a volunteer.'

'Who says I'm a volunteer?'

'Everyone else stepped back.' His arms slid around her and she didn't pull away. Their eyes met and held and then they sank below the surface, eyes wide open as their lips came together. It wasn't quite perfect but Rory was happy to practice. They floated back to the surface.

'That could take a rehearsal.' Kate looked a little breathless.

'Yeah,' Rory said, 'you're a buoyant little thing,' and he could feel the tilt of his mouth as he smiled. 'Let's practice.'

She frowned at him. 'One more, no more.'

This time they kissed before they went under, and Rory side swam with her in his arms to the edge. When his hip hit the bottom he pulled her over so she floated above him and he could look up at her through the water. He could quite happily drown here. Her face moved away as she sat up.

'Enough. We should think about going.'

'The next time you fly over here, will you remember us?'

Remember, Kate thought, and she felt like clutching her chest. This had all been a bad, bad idea.

Rory tried to establish some return to the rapport as they left Xanadu but Kate wasn't playing and he couldn't find any way through her silence.

All he could think was that she was regretting

last night and this morning. He wondered if it would have helped if he'd slowed down and let her get used to the idea that he was back in her life. And wanted to be for good!

They were close to the Pentecost. Kate stared unseeingly out of the window as she thought about what had happened last night.

She'd invited, no, dragged Rory into her room as she'd caught glimpses of the adored and carefree girl she'd been all those years ago. Stupid woman.

Who was she kidding? She had baggage with a capital B and was too screwed up for any sort of relationship. And she needed to concentrate on finding common ground with her father before it was too late.

Rory had his career. Plus he was carrying a few issues himself. She just needed to get the hell out of his arms and back to the real world.

The Pentecost was an anticlimax. The rush

had been through and the river was no deeper than on their way out. The next two hours passed slowly but with no more incidents and finally they drove up the last stretch before Jabiru Township.

Kate looked at the mud at the side of the road. 'I guess you're stuck here until the RFDS can land on the strip.'

Rory frowned. 'Won't you be? Your plane is grounded too.'

She lifted her head. 'I'll drive home. As soon as we get back.'

He tried to control his disappointment. 'Don't go on my account.'

'Why not?'

How could she be so cold after last night? 'It doesn't have to be like this, Kate.'

Her eyes didn't meet his, looked anywhere but his way, just like when he'd first seen her two days ago.

'Yes. It does, Rory.'

He could feel it all slipping away and the panic fluttered like the spinifex at the side of the road as they drove past. Rory ran his hand through his hair. 'You can't deny we shared something special back there at Xanadu.'

Her fingers spread and pressed down on her legs, as if to push away that thought. Still she didn't look at him.

'It's over. Has been for a long time. I'm sorry if I've hurt you, Rory, but I don't want you to come back.'

Those same words from the letter he'd carried all those years. The hurt stirred anger. 'I wish I'd never come back.'

'So do I,' she said quietly.

Rory couldn't give up. He felt that same desolation he'd felt ten years ago. He'd stayed the one night he couldn't avoid in town after Kate had left. Had dinner with Smiley and Sophie, dug for what background they had, and then caught a lift to Derby on a road train early the next morning, like all those years ago, so he could make a flight back from there. Then he drove home from Perth Airport and, without unpacking, he switched on his computer.

He needed to find Fairmont Gardens and a commemorative inscription. Kate needed to grieve and maybe he could get some clue how to help by just seeing where the remains of his son lay.

The next day was a cool autumn day and the Fairmont Gardens were deserted. He crossed the freshly mown grass to the commemorative wall that curved around an enormous bed of roses and the scent was almost heady in its power.

He drew a deep breath and held it, as if imprinting the scent on his memory.

He was standing here for both of them. He didn't know what to expect. How it would affect him. Just knew he had to do this to gain insight into the journey Kate had travelled on her own.

He looked down at the paper printout the custodian had given him with the directions he sought.

Third row down, twenty-six across from the left; his eyes scanned as he counted. Then he saw it.

The plaque, tarnished bronze, six inches by four inches, with raised lettering. *Baby son of Kate Onslow. Lived for a day, 3rd August.*

His son. Rory hadn't expected the rush of sadness that overwhelmed him. Sadness for the little boy who hadn't had the chance to be held by his mother before he'd died. Or his father. He winced at the pain from such a tiny fragment of grief compared to what Kate had had to bury for ten years.

'I'm sorry I wasn't there for you, Cameron.' The quiet words floated up into the branches of the leafy tree overhead.

He turned and gazed over the beautiful gardens, the reminders of other lives that had been and gone, the place that families came to grieve and say goodbye. Then he slid the end of the tiny bouquet he'd brought with him into the slot below.

He thought about Kate—so young, so sick, heartbroken and alone. Kate sending him a letter that must have hurt so much to write and the noble but mistaken reasons she had.

He thought of the day he'd received it and his disbelief. How he'd phoned the housekeeper at Jabiru Station and she'd said Kate wasn't taking calls. And all his letters he'd written that she was destined never to receive.

His parents, working at a new station, the reason for their move now explained, hadn't been able to offer any information on Kate. They had enough trouble of their own trying to adjust.

So he'd stayed, had decided to achieve what he'd set out to do and more, much more. Driven, as Kate said, and for what? To hide the pain that needed Kate. He should have searched for her. Ten years of pain for Kate and him, wasted. He knew that now. And he wasn't wasting any more. He knew where he belonged. What he needed to do.

The card on the bouquet floated in the breeze and he brushed it gently with his finger as he read the words, *With love from Mum and Dad,* and he took a photograph to add to the ones the midwife had confirmed were in the medical records, the grieving parent pack that hospitals kept for years if mementos were refused, not sure if he'd done right to ask.

It was a choice Kate hadn't been given. The hospital had agreed to contact her and ask.

Then he allowed the anguish for everything to float away, to keep the memories—release the pain; their baby, ten years he'd lost with Kate, his sadness and guilt over his parents' early misfortune and, most of all, for Kate's lonely journey.

He understood. He would be there for her and this time she wouldn't turn him away.

It was time to make things happen. He walked away to lay the foundations for his new life. He would give Kate time to come to the same conclusion—he had to believe that time would come—but if it didn't he would make it happen.

Kate drove straight home to Jabiru Homestead after dropping Rory at the Hilton and couldn't help but wonder if she was the same woman who'd left less than forty-eight hours ago. For the first time she considered not selling her family's land after her father died.

Maybe she did deserve a fuller life. She could take over the reins from her father, make changes for the better, maybe some time in the future start a new dynasty of caring and integrity for Jabiru Station and the township.

But first she had to care for the old dynasty.

'Hello, Father.' She looked at him, lying back in the chair overlooking the house yard, a big man brought down by infirmity, his thick white hair still cut short in the military style he preferred and his bushy white brows beetling up at her as he pretended he wasn't in any pain.

'So you're back! Hmmph.' He turned his head away.

'Yes, I am.' She crossed the veranda and picked up his pain relief tablets. 'You haven't taken any pills in two days.'

He glared at her. 'Makes me fuzzy and I don't see what's going on.'

Typical despot. Her voice remained mild. 'There's nothing going on that's worth suffering for.'

He stuck his chin out. 'You can't make me take them.'

'Nope.' Kate shook her head. 'Your choice.' She left that battle but knew he would take them now she was home. He had this thing about the 'family' being alert to what the workers did. And Kate being home meant he could sleep.

She hoped she'd never be that paranoid. 'I went as far as Rainbow's End. They flew Lucy Bolton out from there.'

He thought about that. 'You took long enough, then.'

'The road over the Pentecost was flooded.' She paused and then said deliberately, 'I went with Rory McIver.'

That made him sit up and she saw the agony cross his face with the movement and she felt a moment's regret that she'd startled him. Her father. He must have had some redeeming features when her mother had fallen in love with him but he'd never shown Kate much tenderness.

He pulled himself up, trying not to wince, until he sat straight in the chair. 'That young cockerel. Did he make a pass at you?'

Now that was funny. 'No.' As if her father should worry about that, after all these years.

He sagged a little. 'Good.'

'I made one at him.' Lyle's head snapped up. 'And I told him about the baby.'

'Fool!' He looked away. 'Now, why would you do that? Give him pretensions to glory, knocking up an Onslow.'

Kate winced at the denigration in the comment. This was the only time she could remember when she'd had an equal part in a conversation with her father. And his last comment incensed her. 'If it hadn't been for

Rory and his family I'd have known no love at all after Mother died.'

It was all starting to make sense, though. 'Is that what happened? Did Mother have to marry you? Because of me?'

He poked his finger at her, stabbing the air with each word. 'Your mother was too easy with her ways and then wasn't strong enough to survive out here. She lost my son.'

She shook her head, suddenly sorry for this sad old man she'd never connected with. 'My mother needed more than a roof over her head to live here. And you didn't have a loving bone in your body.'

He sagged back in the chair. 'Too late now.'

Did it have to be? Was there any hope they could salvage something before he was gone?

'Maybe it's not for us. We don't have to fight all the time. It would be handy to have some nice memories of you.'

She came around and crouched down beside him so that he had to look at her. 'Were you ever happy?'

He lifted his head. 'When I thought I'd have a son to carry on with.'

She threw up her hands. 'Get over it.' She stared at him. 'Rory could have been that son but you blew it.'

'That camp trash? I'd rather leave it to a dogs' home.'

She glared right into his face. 'I might sell it to a dogs' home.'

'You're no child of mine.' It was more of a mutter than a statement and they both knew it wasn't true.

She sat back, her humour restored. 'Unfortunately, I do have a stubborn and determined side that I've inherited from you, but you're too bitter and twisted to see it.'

He didn't say anything. His mouth moved but

didn't open to speak. She gave him another few seconds but he turned away.

She sighed. 'Goodnight, Father. I'll send John in to help you to bed, then I'll bring the rest of your medications.'

The next morning, Kate opened her eyes and stared at the familiar plaster rose on the ceiling above her bed. Since she'd first arrived back to nurse her father, despite her determination to sell, she couldn't help her feeling of belonging to Jabiru.

Yet this morning it was not the same. Her father had never really cared for her—it was out in plain words, lost in his all enveloping grief at not having a son to inherit. Well, he deserved that she wanted to sell.

But she didn't know what she wanted. The idea of waking every morning, like today, alone in the middle of this vastness, wasn't that different from waking alone in a big city like Perth.

At least here she could be useful to people like Lucy, and the Aboriginal women who sometimes needed help to birth, or the man with the croc bite.

She'd be an orphan, no relatives that she knew of, no friends her own age except Sophie and Smiley. Was that what she wanted?

At breakfast her father looked more subdued but without that patina of pain he'd worn yesterday, so he was taking his tablets. He seemed to have thawed slightly towards her and she wondered if anything she'd said yesterday had perhaps made him think.

'You said you're determined and stubborn,' he growled, 'I'm guessing you'd have to be to put up with me.' He looked at her from under his brows. 'And why do you?'

She half laughed. 'Because that's what family do.'

'How would you know?' He sniffed.

'I read about it.' She looked him over. 'How are you today?'

He glared at her. 'Old.'

She raised her eyebrows. 'Here's the good news—it doesn't last for ever.'

He gave a bark of laughter and she nearly fell off her chair in surprise. 'You should have stuck up for yourself years ago. I like you better.'

Okay for him because he was old and able to say what he thought. 'It would have been helpful if you'd given me a hint.'

'Hmmph.'

She looked at him for a moment, fleetingly sad for the impending loss of this tiny rapport. 'I'll see you later. I have to go to work.'

He narrowed his eyes and then shook his head angrily, once. 'Why? They can get other people to do that menial stuff you do.'

He really didn't get it. She'd fight every day

against ever becoming that selfish. 'The menial stuff I do saved a baby and mother's life. If there had been someone around when I was Lucy's age you'd have had a grandson to leave your precious station to.' She stood up. 'I'll be back tonight.'

As she walked away she accepted that they might talk a little more civilly to each other, and even on a rare occasion have a laugh over some incident on the station, but it was never going to be warm and fuzzy.

In Kate's mind, as well, there was always going to be a rift from his unfeeling stand over her pregnancy.

Over the next few weeks Kate flew between Jabiru Station and the township and each day she settled more into the idea of staying in the Kimberley.

On the Friday, three weeks after she'd left,

Lucy Bolton and her mother returned with her baby and came to visit Kate.

The young woman glowed with health and her tiny baby already was filling out into the cutest cherub.

'How's it all going, Lucy?' Kate said, but she could see everything was going well.

'Cool. Missy eats a lot but she sleeps straight after so that's easy.'

Kate checked Lucy's blood pressure and the readings had returned to normal. 'We'll still have to watch you if you decide on more children.'

Lucy laughed. 'Not just yet, thanks.'

'Congratulations on being a nana, Mary.' Kate smiled at the older woman. 'You look like you're loving it.'

Mary smoothed Missy's hair. 'I'm very lucky. And how's that Rory McIver? I nearly fell over when I saw he was your driver. Hasn't he turned into a handsome man?'

Kate plastered a smile on her face. 'He's back in Perth in his high profile job for the Ambulance. He even sent the clinic a satellite phone, though technically I'm not supposed to know it was him.' She pretended to whisper. 'They told me at the post office it was from him. So I guess he's still thinking of Jabiru.'

That wasn't all he'd sent. He'd sent a letter to say he'd been to see their baby's grave and a photo and, a day later, a short letter from the hospital had arrived. It had taken her days to ring for the grieving parent package to be sent. Still she waited.

Mary gave Kate a tiny nudge and Kate blinked and remembered where she was.

'It must have been nice to see him after all these years,' Mary said and Kate tried not to see the wink. 'You two still in contact, then?'

'Mum!' Lucy nudged her mother out of the way and frowned her to silence. 'That's between Kate and Rory,' and she took Kate's hand in both of hers. 'Thank you for everything, Kate. You were wonderful and I would have been terrified if you hadn't been here for me.' Lucy hugged her and went on, 'They said in Derby I could have lost my darling Missy if I'd got much worse.'

Kate hugged her back. 'You're so welcome and I'm glad Missy is fine. Drop in and see me any time.'

'So you're staying on at Jabiru?' Mary asked.

'For a while.' Kate thought about it. She had decided. 'Yes. For a long while.'

After work Kate called in again to the post office and this time the postmistress handed her a package. Kate thanked her carefully, because suddenly her mouth wasn't working too well. Her body felt as if it were covered in thin ice and she stumbled stiffly out of the tiny shop like an old woman as she clutched the large white envelope to her breast.

She walked blindly to her car but when she reached it she had to turn her face up to catch the afternoon sun to warm her cheeks. 'How ridiculous. To be cold when the day's hitting thirty-seven degrees,' she admonished herself, needing the sound of her own voice and the heat to soak into her skin and into her heart before she unlocked the car door to climb in.

She leant back on the seat and the package lay in her lap, bulky yet light. She had a fair idea what it would contain because she'd prepared just such packages for other broken-hearted families in her midwifery training.

She didn't open it—couldn't open it—and a tiny voice inside her head suggested that there was someone else who should be there when she did.

Instead, she opened her overnight bag that

she kept for emergencies and slipped the package in amongst her clothes. Maybe later.

Her father was worse when she got home and she put the envelope away for a time when she had emotions to spare.

There was an improvement in rapport between Kate and her father as Lyle became weaker and more resigned to eternal rest.

Kate could feel the ball of resentment she'd held against him slowly unravelling as he talked to her more.

'Your mother was a beautiful woman,' he said one morning, 'and you're not bad yourself.'

'I'll try not to let your effusive compliments go to my head,' Kate said, straight-faced, and he shot a look at her before he actually laughed out loud. Then he sucked his breath in as the pain bit.

When he had his breathing under control

again Kate asked the questions she'd always wanted to ask. 'Why were you so cold to me?'

He avoided her eyes. 'Was I? Don't know any different,' he said. 'My own mother died when I was two. That's how I was brought up. When my son died with your mother I knew you needed to be tough to run this place. No room for namby-pamby cry babies.'

Kate shook her head. 'This place is a well-oiled machine and kindness isn't a weakness.' She looked him in the eye. 'It's a strength.'

For once he didn't bluster. 'Maybe I got it wrong but that's all I knew. It might have been different if your mother had lived.'

'Maybe you should have married again.'

'Hmmph. I don't have to. It's your job to ensure the succession.'

She gathered their plates. 'You might have blown it there. I'm not looking for a husband. Are there any cousins or relatives anywhere?'

'You'd better sell it to the dogs' home.' He was watching her like a hawk and she doubted he missed her frown. No, she didn't think she could do that now. Every day she felt more like she belonged, except for the emptiness at night, but she guessed that would never go away.

CHAPTER TEN

A MONTH after Rory had left, Kate landed on the strip of her father's property and saw a dust-covered Range Rover waiting beside her own farm vehicle. Somehow she knew it was Rory.

In that moment she panicked and looked at the fuel gauge. All she wanted to do was dip the wing into a turn and circle back the way she'd come, to run, hide, but the sensible pilot inside her head disagreed. Land, the pilot said.

There was fuel to spare, but not much, and Kate always listened to the pilot. As she touched down the roaring of the engine echoed in her head and she tried to block out the questions.

Why had he come back? Why now, when

her father was so ill? What should she do? How should she act? She'd be caught in the middle again.

The plane taxied to a stop and she looked across as the propeller began to wind down. At least he was on his own and she didn't have to pretend it wasn't a shock to see him. And he looked amazing.

Damn. It wasn't fair. She was dishevelled, exhausted from the broken sleeps with her father as he became more ill, and wretched.

The wind blew his shirt against his muscular chest, the one she wanted to rest her head against, and he lifted his hand to hold his Akubra firmly on his head, hiding the thick dark hair she loved.

Loved! The truth crashed into her as if she'd landed her plane into a fence instead of kissing the airstrip and parking normally. She'd been miserable because she'd missed Rory. Because Rory's presence was life and promise and the future—her future—and she'd been too stubborn and frightened to take the risk when he'd come back after all these years and she'd thought that chance was gone.

It should have been her landing at his back door to say she'd got it wrong. Should have been her asking for forgiveness. Her explaining she loved Rory as much, if not more than ten years ago and would he please never leave her again.

All the fruitless mental discussion of how it was better she'd seen him and could forget the past. The exhaustion and misery of the last month.

What a fool she'd been.

It was all dirt and lies and bull dust. She loved Rory McIver with all her heart and soul and always would. She just needed the guts to tell him!

She shaded her eyes as she climbed out and then jumped down to the ground in front of him.

'How are you, Kate?' He saw beneath her bravado to the young woman within and suddenly her bravery was gone.

She couldn't do it. What if it was too late? Tiredness hit her like a tsunami, flattened her, bowled her off her feet so in her mind she bobbed with indecision. She didn't look at him as she walked to her vehicle. 'Tired.' Such a small, spineless voice. She disgusted herself. 'How are you, Rory? Have you been to the house?'

'Yes.' His quiet, gravelly voice, low with compassion.

That pulled her up. 'Spoken with my father?'

'Yes.'

This time she looked straight into his face. Questioning. Dreading the answer. 'And you're both still alive?'

'He was when I left him.' His voice lowered. 'Just.'

She sagged. She didn't know how she was

going to get through that either. 'I know. He hasn't long. He's just an old man who's made some wrong choices along the way and he has to live, and die, with those choices.' Like she did. She looked at Rory. 'In the last month I've come to terms with that. He's still my father.'

Rory smiled at her. Undemanding. Empathetic. Her Rory. 'I'm glad. I'm here because I'd like to stay with you until the end, Kate. Be here for you. Like I wasn't before. When Cameron died.'

She felt the tears build behind her eyes and they felt heavier than usual. But she never cried.

That was why he'd come back. How had he known she'd dreaded being alone when it happened? Technically, though, she'd have people around her—the housekeeper she'd only met two months ago, who didn't normally live-in, the manager, the yard man, John, the stockmen, the drivers and overseers. Not on her own—but alone.

He wouldn't stay. He had his important position to go back to.

'How long have you got?'

'As long as you need me.' That calm, reassuring Rory voice.

Fine words. 'What about your high-powered job?'

He shook his head. 'You're my family. As long as you need me.'

He'd do that for her? Risk everything he'd worked for to hold her hand? Be with her at the end and comfort her? No one else had ever worried about her like Rory.

And she couldn't even risk saying she loved him?

It was as if the sky cleared and the dark clouds of the last few weeks were blown away from over her head. Maybe forgiving her father had helped. Maybe knowing there was a time in the not too distant future when she could meet her lost son—if only on paper. But suddenly those restraining shackles had gone. This was all about her and Rory. So what was she going to do?

Was she going to pretend she hadn't just had the biggest brain snap in history and wait for him to decide their fate?

Or was she going to take her future in her own hands and lift her head and meet his eyes and tell him she loved him more than she could believe was possible for one woman to love a man?

It was a terrifying thought, but not as terrifying as him walking away without the truth leaving her lips.

She looked into Rory's caring eyes, this tall and straight, fabulous man of her dreams, who had never forgotten her and she spoke the truth. 'I love you, Rory McIver. With all my heart. I always will. Thank you for coming back to be with me.'

Kate felt the tears sting and then they welled. She struggled to hold them back and then realised she didn't have to. Amazingly, dampness spilled over onto her cheeks. For the first time in ten years, Kate Onslow cried. She stepped into Rory's open arms and he lifted her to him and kissed her cheeks before he set her down to cradle her against his chest.

She cried great gulping, soul-freeing sobs, and she cried quiet, whispering weeps until his shirt was sticking to her face with dampness and then she pulled away and gave him the first of many watery smiles.

She wiped her cheeks with her fingers until he pushed her hands aside and patted the tear trails himself with the big white handkerchief he'd tried to give her.

'I bet—' she sniffed '—you didn't expect that tropical storm,' and she snatched the handkerchief from him and inelegantly blew her nose before she crumpled the wet cloth into a ball and jammed it into her khaki trousers.

'I'd say it's about time.' Then he kissed her. Inexpertly at first because she hadn't expected it and then perfectly, amazingly, healingly until there was no doubt that her own revelation in the plane was matched by his.

His words caressed her as he spoke into her ear. 'I love you, Kate. I'm here for you. Always.'

Once started, she couldn't stop. It was time to open herself to the love he promised.

'I love you, too,' she said. 'I was a fool to push you away when you came back. I've missed you so much this last month, but goodness knows how long it would have taken me to be brave enough to come and tell you. Thank you for taking that risk.'

'Again,' he teased.

'Again.' She wiped her eyes.

He squeezed her shoulders. 'Have I ever told you everything would work out fine?'

She looked up at him. Her hero. 'For years.'

'And that's how long I'll be here. For years and years and years.' He captured her hand and kissed her palm. 'For ever. My darling Kate, I've always loved you, never more than now.'

He pulled a tiny box from his pocket and it sat there in his palm, daring her to open the lid. 'Will you marry me? This time?'

She looked at him and then the box and, as he had so many years ago, he took the ring and slid it on her finger.

The most exquisite pink Argyle diamond ring; the size of the central stone took her breath away, but it was the much smaller diamond beside it that brought more tears to her eyes. 'My original stone from the ring you gave me? You kept it?'

She looked from the ring to Rory. This man

she'd cut from her life so many years ago had never given up and she shuddered to think of how close she'd been to losing that chance.

Later that night, when Kate had seen to her father's comfort and most of the lights were out in the homestead, she found Rory on the swing on the veranda watching the night sky as he waited for her. Still waiting.

He made room beside him and slid his arm around her shoulders as they sat hip to hip in the dark. The moon shone from behind a cloud and the sound of a night bird echoed eerily over the silver paddocks.

'How are you?' he asked quietly.

She snuggled in against him. 'So much better now you're here.'

He stroked her arm. 'I'm not going anywhere.'

She pouted but he couldn't see so she patted his leg. 'I was thinking we could go to bed.'

'Are you trying to seduce me again? Under your father's roof?' She could hear the smile in his voice.

A flicker of heat curled in her stomach. 'Serve him right.'

'I think not,' came the measured voice of her beloved from the darkness beside her.

'Rory McIver!' She couldn't believe he'd refused her offer. She'd been fantasising about him all day. Had watched his mouth as he talked, the way he held his head as he walked, and stared at the sprinkling of dark hairs in the vee of his shirt so much she could have plotted their pattern. Had waited, very impatiently, to relive those magic hours they'd shared at Xanadu.

'No, my wanton little midwife. I want to marry you first this time. Tonight I want to dance with you in the moonlight. Hold you under the same stars that I held you all those years ago. Then fall asleep, just holding you until you are my wife. Does that sound so bad?'

The wedding was intimate, beautiful, and held at Jabiru Homestead very quickly. Smiley and Sophie were attendants and even the bedridden Lyle seemed resigned to their marriage.

Kate never knew what Rory had told him but she'd seen the grudging respect her father paid to Rory now.

Her world was in harmony. That night Kate slept, sated, and with a soft smile curving her lips. Safe and finally at peace in the place she belonged—in Rory's arms.

When Lyle Onslow died he was put to rest beside his wife and infant son, in the family plot on the hill above the homestead.

Beside him stood a tiny angel, in memory of Cameron Onslow-McIver, 3rd August.

Kate stood in the windswept paddock and gazed out at the land she loved, at the land Lyle had taught her to love, and thought, this is right.

Forgiveness came from loving. Forgiveness was healing all on its own and her love had come full circle.

Life could move on.

One year later

'You said you'd never ask me to do something I didn't want to.' Kate tossed her head against the plastic-covered pillow in the shower. 'I can't do it. I want to go home.'

If they'd been anywhere but here, the birthing centre at Perth General, Rory would have given in, plucked her up into his arms and carried her all the way back to Jabiru.

But she'd told him about this. The end of the first stage of labour. Transition. He said what he'd been told to.

'I know. I love you. You're doing beautifully.' And he kissed her and held her hand and she ground her wedding ring into his already painful fingers until suddenly her eyes opened wide, startled yet intent.

'I have to push.'

'Hallelujah,' he said under his breath because he'd been ready to scream for a transfer to a labour ward and an epidural, anything to stop the pain for the love of his life.

'Oh, my,' she said as the sensations took over.

'Remember the breathing. Calm breathing.' He couldn't believe he was saying this, but then again he was doing it too, and the breathing had been the only thing that had got him through this. He'd been breathing his heart out for what seemed like forever.

His feet ached in his new leather boots, both boots as soaking wet as the bottoms of his jeans, but Kate had needed the shower as soon as they'd arrived and he hadn't had time to change.

The steam from the shower had Kate's hair sticking to her forehead and he reached over and offered her a sip of water through the straw.

Kate sipped urgently and then spat the straw out as the next contraction started and hastily he put the cup down. He still found labour very stressful.

The midwife watched them both and smiled. She didn't say much, this old bird, he thought fleetingly as he smiled back, but she'd been just like Kate had been when Lucy had birthed. Calm, unflappable, unlike the way he was feeling.

Oh, my God, he could see the baby's head. The midwife put the Doppler low over Kate's stomach and the clop, clop of his baby's heart rate filled the bathroom. Soon—very soon—he would meet their child.

'Nice and gentle,' Rory said because he remembered Kate had said that to Lucy all that time ago and nobody else said anything. He looked around.

With only the three of them here it was suddenly incredibly peaceful. Kate was totally focused on the job at hand now, with the warm shower water cascading over her shoulders like that day at Xanadu and the waterfalls in the gorge.

The midwife was prepared and patient and he was the only one talking now. It seemed he couldn't keep his mouth shut. He clamped his lips together and realised their song from their teenage years was playing in the background.

Then slowly, crease by wrinkled forehead skin crease, their baby began to birth until a thick mop of damp hair and a squashed little face spun to stare at him.

'Rest one hand under the bottom shoulder as it comes out and put your other hand on the top shoulder,' the midwife said quietly.

He was holding it. He looked up at Kate and she was staring through him as she concentrated.

Suddenly he was holding all of him… her…he didn't know which…and the baby was as slippery as a little eel and he juggled and skidded it up Kate's belly until her hands closed around it and she searched for his face. His. Her husband. Rory's.

'Oh, my stars,' she breathed out. 'Hello, baby. A boy or a girl? What is it?' Kate was still looking at him, unable to believe it was over and she held their baby in her arms between her breasts.

'It's a…' Rory lifted one leg and tried to see but it was all too hard to peer through the tears in his eyes and the baby skidded and folded up like a puppy. The midwife's hands came in and she tilted the baby so he could look properly.

His heart swelled. 'We have a daughter.

Jasmine.' He looked at Kate and tears ran down his face. 'She's incredibly beautiful, like her mother.'

MEDICAL™

Large Print

Titles for the next six months...

September

THE DOCTOR'S LOST-AND-FOUND BRIDE	Kate Hardy
MIRACLE: MARRIAGE REUNITED	Anne Fraser
A MOTHER FOR MATILDA	Amy Andrews
THE BOSS AND NURSE ALBRIGHT	Lynne Marshall
NEW SURGEON AT ASHVALE A&E	Joanna Neil
DESERT KING, DOCTOR DADDY	Meredith Webber

October

THE NURSE'S BROODING BOSS	Laura Iding
EMERGENCY DOCTOR AND CINDERELLA	Melanie Milburne
CITY SURGEON, SMALL TOWN MIRACLE	Marion Lennox
BACHELOR DAD, GIRL NEXT DOOR	Sharon Archer
A BABY FOR THE FLYING DOCTOR	Lucy Clark
NURSE, NANNY...BRIDE!	Alison Roberts

November

THE SURGEON'S MIRACLE	Caroline Anderson
DR DI ANGELO'S BABY BOMBSHELL	Janice Lynn
NEWBORN NEEDS A DAD	Dianne Drake
HIS MOTHERLESS LITTLE TWINS	Dianne Drake
WEDDING BELLS FOR THE VILLAGE NURSE	Abigail Gordon
HER LONG-LOST HUSBAND	Josie Metcalfe